MALLORY

MALLORY

by

Margaret Gunning

TURNSTONE PRESS

Mallory
copyright © Margaret Gunning 2005

Turnstone Press
Artspace Building
607-100 Arthur Street
Winnipeg, MB
R3B 1H3 Canada
www.TurnstonePress.com

Turnstone Press gratefully acknowledges the assistance of The Canada
Council for the Arts, the Manitoba Arts Council, the Government of
Canada through the Book Publishing Industry Development Program and
the Government of Manitoba through the Department of Culture, Heritage
and Tourism, Arts Branch, for our publishing activities.

 Canada Council   Conseil des Arts
for the Arts   du Canada

 MANITOBA arts COUNCIL
CONSEIL DES DU MANITOBA

Canadä

Cover design: Doowah Design
Interior design: Sharon Caseburg
Cover photo courtesy of Margaret Gunning.
Printed and bound in Canada by Friesens for Turnstone Press.

Library and Archives Canada Cataloguing in Publication

Gunning, Margaret, 1954-
  Mallory / by Margaret Gunning.

ISBN 0-88801-311-6

  I. Title.

PS8563.U5754M34 2005   C813'.6   C2005-904042-4

To the memory of my brother, Arthur Thomas Burton (1949–1980).

"The gold is in the dark."
—Carl Jung

MALLORY

PROLOGUE:MANWOMAN

Mallory is fat.

God is she fat. So fat you couldn't stand it. But fat would not be so bad. There is the matter of the beard, a skinny collection of little hairs she can twist into a spindly tuft at the bottom of her chin. Seventeen hairs at last count. And her arms. They are so gangly they hang all the way down to the floor.

The dark frames of her glasses barely contain the sweaty thick lenses that make her eyes swim like two vague and faraway fish. One dense eyebrow punctuates her face like an accent scored over a vowel sound from some heavy Slavic dialect.

There is a smell to her too, but that Mallory will barely bring herself to think about. When people notice her, which they hardly ever do, they look for bulges in her crotch, though two breasts swell like dough on a torso built like a top, whittled at the waist and swollen at the chest.

Mallory looks in the glass and a gorilla looks back. She can see where all the words come from, poison words. *Sucky*. Suck-of-the-world. Bitch. Cunt. And the worst, *manwoman*. This monster is folded away in a body slight as a twelve-year-old's, lanky in black turtleneck and black stretch pants with seams sewn down the front. This is her invisible self, the self she slips about in all day, innocuous as a goldfish. The hulking animal in the glass is the one everyone can see under her clothes, an open secret.

She rakes her bleedy bitten fingernail-stumps down the glass to erase the big Mallory, the bad. It is November and Mallory has a poppy on her chest, a round bit of red cardboard secured by a pin. She takes the pin carefully out of the poppy, turns it between her fingers for a moment.

Jab. *Jab*. With the small stab, the welling of rubies on her skin, pressure seems to escape from her body. She is right-sized now, not monster Mallory but little Mallory, Mallory the good. This is why she keeps her arms covered, so no one will see. It is her refuge, a black sort of peace like a rose coated in crude oil. A terrible blooming. The bad is outside her now. For now. Exhausted peace comes like the peace after throwing up, after crying for hours. A faint sort of peace like almost passing out, or too much Benylin cough syrup drunk straight from the bottle.

Peace like a buzzing in the ears.

Peace like a deathly plunge into sleep.

PART I:
MALLORY

1962

Mallory, eight, sits on the tree stump with a magnifying glass.

Once, the tree had been an elm. Mallory couldn't remember it. To her, it had always been a stump, a place to sit in the backyard. Fungus grows out of it, and moss. Inside it seethes with life, as all rotten things do.

Mallory sits on the stump with her magnifying glass and tries to get the ants to slow down. Ants always hurry. They always seem to have a sort of crazed sense of purpose. They remind her of the adults. She wonders how they can be so sure. What gives them the authority. Mallory wonders if their authority comes from God. She also wonders what God is.

An ant pauses and Mallory tries to focus the rays of the sun through the glass. But quickly it runs on. Getting impatient, she finds a dry leaf, holds the magnifying glass over it, angles it carefully. The tiniest pinprick forms on the leaf, a black pinhole that spreads with a small plume of white smoke.

Mallory loves to burn holes. If an ant would stay still, she would try to concentrate the white-hot spot of light on its body, to see what would happen. Mallory is not cruel, just curious. But she can't make an ant stay, so she never finds out.

Mallory finds small fallen birds in the grass every spring, or they find her, fluffy balls of need keening to her. She is thought odd, her friends find her odd, to be so absorbed in small helpless things. But Mallory just is, not standing outside nature to observe, but moving in and through it. She looks down more than she looks up. She will follow a centipede down the street. She will dry the caps of wild mushrooms in the sun on the elm stump until they are nearly the texture of china.

Sometimes she climbs the sour-cherry tree beside the white

7

picket fence that divides the Mardlings' backyard from their neighbours'. The Voortmans are from Holland and they keep pigeons in a coop. When Mallory climbs the cherry tree, she can easily drop down to the ground on the other side of the fence and run over to the pigeon coop.

The sound they make is some kind of heaven, a ruffling, muddling, churling sound, fat and soft as a pillow. She even knows the pigeons' names. *Browntop. Blackwing. Whiteboy.* Throw a handful of dried peas and corn on the pigeon-coop floor and soon will come a circling, pecking chaos, iridescent necks bobbing and flashing. Round eyes, pink feet, fat motherly breasts. She loves them more than she can stand.

Then Mallory sees Mrs. Voortman stick her head out the back door and yell in her shrill voice: "Annie and Suze! Come an' get your yackets!" Anika and Susan Voortman, skipping out in the front yard, trudge reluctantly to the door for their coats.

"Hi, Mallory."

"Hi, Annie."

"Don't feed the pigeons."

"I didn't."

"I saw you, you know."

"What?"

"I saw you with that *bird*." Annie makes it all sound so stupid.

"So?"

"So, it's just going to die. My brother says so."

"How do you know?"

"It's got lice on it."

"Does not."

"Does so. Does your mother know you have it?"

Mallory wants to get out of there. Annie is the oldest of six. Bossy. Born with a sense of being at the top of the pecking order. It even affects the way she holds herself. Mallory slumps, a lastborn, absorbing the fact she was an afterthought, if not a mistake.

"You wanna see?" Mallory knows she has her now.

Annie pretends not to be interested, but follows her over to the cherry tree. "Brian says it's a stupid-looking bird," she says, landing on the ground in Mallory's yard. "Just a starling."

"C'mon." The two head for the back door of the house, which leads down into the basement, Mallory's treasure-place, a dark, seeping place full of shivery secrets. The house is very old and once belonged to rich people. There is a sort of cupboard called a dumb waiter where servants used to put the dirty dishes, now used as a laundry chute. The heating system is ancient and bulky, with big curving furnace pipes like the intestines of a dragon. And the best, the most secret place, is just a little room in the corner with no floor at all, only dirt. No one ever told Mallory what a root cellar was, so she has no idea why it is here.

"Come see." In the root cellar is a big cardboard box with holes poked in it. Annie tries to hide her fascination. Mallory lifts the lid.

The baby bird huddles in an old towel, its black eyes stunned.

"It's gonna die," Annie says, kneeling on the dirt.

"Is not."

"Your last one died."

"It wouldn't eat. This one eats."

"Your mum's going to find out."

"Don't tell."

"Give me your horse book, then."

"No." Mallory will not surrender her old handed-down copy of *Misty of Chincoteague* for anything.

"I'll tell."

"You can have my Cinderella slippers." Mallory and Annie both have birthdays in February, only one day apart, and sometimes go to each other's houses for birthday dinners, when they're speaking. On their last birthdays when they turned eight, they had each given the other the same gift, a pair of pink plastic high-heeled slippers held on with strips of elastic, with elegant gold sparkles embedded in the plastic. The heels on Annie's had broken the first day. Mallory never wears hers.

"I want them now."

"Tomorrow."

"Now!"

"Poop! Mum's coming." The two of them race for the steps and nearly knock Mrs. Mardling over as she trundles down the stairs.

"Nola, I mean, Mallory. Supper's almost ready." This happens nearly every day. Mallory's mum calls her by her older sister's name. She should be used to it.

"*Okay.*"

"What kind of tone is that?"

Annie smirks. It makes Mallory furious. The two escape to the backyard.

"You're not going to tell," says Mallory.

"Give me the slippers."

"Tomorrow."

Mrs. Voortman saves the day by calling Annie in to supper.

MALLORY IN PHYSICS CLASS

Mallory, older. Writing a poem under her desk. Sloppily, because she can't see the poem and must go by feel. She knows it is a bad poem, but is only writing it with half her brain. At the front of the class, Mr. Heersma talks about the periodic table of elements.

Sodium = Na. Silver = Ag. It makes no sense, a cryptic language. This fascinates Mallory, though she does poorly in chemistry and physics. On her report card, Mr. Heersma notes, "Has a definite aptitude, but does not apply herself. Her mind appears to be elsewhere."

in my element
in physics class
you enter the dream
you the teller of my mysteries

She dares not look at Bruce except in her peripheral vision. This makes him more exciting. Bruce will not look at Mallory, who is wearing her usual black, her long sleeves in all weather. This is her costume of invisibility, and it almost works. He cannot know about the scars, pricks, burns, picked scabs. They are her secret.

in my element
here in this class
you my blue eyed wanderer
keeper of the pieces of my soul

Mr. Heersma begins to talk about Krebb's Cycle. Mallory wonders how often he fucks his wife. *Fucks*. She knows certain

things because she has pained herself to find out. Knows because
she has dug out her parents' copy of *Ideal Marriage* while they are
away at choir practice. Knows about another book, even better
because it is from Europe and has pictures in it, called *ABZ*. This
one is Mallory's favourite, an encyclopaedia of sex, full of strange,
forbidden practices, things married people do in Italy and France,
with exotic names like *cunnilingus* and *fellatio*. These discoveries
make her fizz and swell where no one can see. Bruce, oblivious,
inspires reams of poetry. Bad poetry. These also no one will see,
for Mallory burns them.

you my blue eyed
tale teller, teller of my secrets
you my

VICTOR

Victor gets away with anything, for he is the one Mum and Dad like the most. Is it his looks, Mallory wonders. He isn't exactly handsome, but his lips are bow-shaped, his eyes a liquid brown, his teeth very white, and people like to look at him. Too, he is smart. He also did the tests Mallory had to do before they sent her clear across town to go to the special school.

Victor is a magician because he can make things happen, make people come. He never tries to make a friend; friends just appear. They don't come to Mallory, who only has friends for a little while, maybe an afternoon. Then they don't want to be seen with a girl like her.

Victor takes a potato, just a plain potato out of the bin in the pantry, washes it off and takes a drinking straw, an ordinary drinking straw made of plastic. He holds the potato in one hand and the drinking straw in the other and then, all of a sudden, *shoop*— the straw is through the potato, clean through. Magic. Then he removes the straw and the little tube of raw potato in the centre of it. When he has enough of these, he turns on the Bunsen burner in the basement, Mallory's magic place. He takes a gob of Fluffo shortening from Mum's kitchen and melts it down over the Bunsen burner and cooks the small tubes of potato. Then he puts salt on them. "Shoestrings," he says, sometimes letting Mallory have some.

Victor takes chunks of lead—no one knows how he gets these. Lead = Pb. *Plumbum*. He melts the lead over the Bunsen burner until it pours silver like the mercury the two of them love to play with out of broken thermometers. Takes the melted lead and dumps it into cold water where it freezes in odd, sculpted shapes, some delicate as hoarfrost, others twisted like viscera.

Victor gets hashish, no one knows from where, either. This makes Mallory's Donovan records sing magic, expand. The whole world expands. Expands and expands. That night she might not hurt herself. Might forget the constant ache in the core of her, might sink for a while into a brief and blessed numbness.

MALLORY, FOUR

Mallory is being led through a completely empty house. This is where they will live. A big echoing cavernous house with high ceilings and no furniture. Mallory believes they will sit on the floor, sleep on the floor. No one has explained it otherwise. The kitchen looks ancient, full of dark wood and smelling musty, like at Gramma's house. But this place also smells different, old-new, fresh paint slathered over yellowy cracked plaster.

This memory is fixed in Mallory's mind forever by several events. There is something they call *sputnik*. No one explains that, either. Mallory believes it must be a new style of spudnut. A spudnut is a large round doughnut slathered in pink, white or chocolate icing. You buy them at The Spudnut Shop.

Then they are climbing up on the roof of her father's store at night to look at the doughnut. It circles in the sky and makes a sound. *Beep beep beep beep beep.* Mallory doesn't hear anything and doesn't see anything, in spite of Victor's telescope that he ordered out of the back of a comic book, the *Jimmy Olsen Annual.*

Then there is the stick. Mallory is not sure how it got in her but it hurt, bad. Victor put his hand over her mouth when she cried. *Shhhh, Mum will hear.* But Mum doesn't hear, and if she does, she doesn't come. No one ever comes. The end of the popsicle stick looks funny sticking out of her secret place, the place she is not supposed to talk about or touch. When Victor pulls it out, it's streaked with her blood.

No one explains this, either.

Then it happens for the first time, when Mallory is walking along the street holding her mother's hand. An older girl, maybe eight, looks her up and down. With a sour face like her mother makes when she washes her diaphragm in the sink.

"You look like a *boy*," the girl says. Mallory doesn't know what a diaphragm is, but she does see her mother washing something round and brown in the morning. She sees everything.

GRAMMA

Then Gramma has to come to live with them. She is taking spells. And the new house has extra rooms. Mallory's mum must look after her, and it is a worry. Mallory can sit on Gramma's lap and play with the soft fold of skin under her chin. She is not supposed to do that, but Gramma doesn't mind. Gramma smells sort of like pee and says things like, "Oh bless her heart."

Gramma now has trouble walking, and puts her hand on Mallory's head to steady herself. Mallory is a living cane. Sometimes she stands up and a big bunch of water lands on the floor. This is a worry. Mallory doesn't quite understand it. There are pads called Modess in the linen cupboard. They must be for the pee. Mallory is not supposed to look at them, but she does look at them, often.

Mallory's mother doesn't like her. She knows this, has always known. Mallory came about in the worst way. This is the earliest scene: there was an egg, just like every month of the year, and about a jillion sperm, like most nights, and one of these sperm, the wrong one, wiggled its way under the round brown thing and wormed itself through the casing of the egg. Then things began to happen and happen and happen, as if energy had been shot out of a cannon. It knows how to happen, has always known, but this time a small child was the result, a girl child who looked different from the very beginning, a fundamental mistake.

The doctor has a little doubt when she is first held up in the air. "It's a . . . wait a minute." That isn't the right thing to say, at all. But Mallory's mother doesn't know what a clitoris is. Has never heard of the term, and thinks that the doctor is being inappropriate in mentioning it, if not downright dirty.

She is told to go home and raise her new baby as a normal little girl.

Mallory knows she has a button. To touch it feels almost better than anything, but as with most things that feel good, she also knows she is not supposed to touch it, even though she has never been told. Shortly after her birth they talked about an operation, a "procedure" they would perform when she was five or six to make her genitalia appear more normal, but it never happened. Mum was too embarrassed to talk to a doctor about it, so she let it go by. No one will see it anyway.

Gramma loves Mallory the way Mallory loves Bloopy, her blue dog. Bloopy has a zipper in his stomach. When Bloopy was new, three puppies fit inside the zipper. Winken, Blinken and Nod.

Bloopy is ugly and has no fur and smells stale and is shaped like a foetus from being squeezed. Mallory can get on Gramma's lap and snuggle her body in to fit the old woman's collapsed chest. It is a perfect fit.

IN THE NAME OF THE FATHER

They are hanging out in Victor's bedroom like they have so many times before. Mallory slumps in his office chair, the one that rolls on casters and turns all the way around. In black like always, her small girlish tits the only topography on an otherwise flat, skinny body. Victor has been reading *The Tibetan Book of the Dead*. A large black and white poster of W.C. Fields in a top hat holding a fan of cards looks down on them from the bedroom wall.

"I know what it is," Victor says. He's pouring a violently pink-coloured powder into his mouth from a straw.

"Know what what is?"

"Why all that stuff keeps happening." He works his mouth around the sour-sweet, saliva-producing powder. "The lights going on and off and stuff. And the TV going off and on by itself."

"Dad said it's a power surge."

"Nah. It's in you." Victor tosses the empty straw into the garbage pail, then opens his bottom drawer and reaches inside. There are over a hundred Pixy Stix in the drawer, every flavour there is. He offers one to Mallory and she shakes her head. She has barely eaten today, trying to lose weight, to get back down to ninety pounds.

"It's a demon," he says.

"Shit. You've been reading that stupid book again."

"Hell, it's in the Bible. Practically on every page in the gospels, Jesus drives out demons. Sends them into pigs and stuff."

"Too weird."

"I know about the marks on your arms," he says.

Mallory doesn't say anything. Her eyes are huge with shock. She thought no one knew.

"I know what's making you do that stuff."

There is no way in the world anyone could ever know what makes her do that stuff.

"It's a demon. Or maybe a whole bunch of demons, I dunno. Wanna smoke up?"

Mallory nods. Her insides are hollow with terror. But there is the thought that the numb misery inside her might just have a cause. Something like hope struggles to awaken in her. Victor rummages in another drawer and pulls out hashish in small brown chunks, and a three-dot Brigham pipe covered in tinfoil. He sucks on the pipe as he lights the bits of hash sitting on top of the foil, then hands Mallory the top of a pen. She sucks air through it, drawing in the smoke, holding it in her lungs for as long as she can.

Holding it and holding it.

Wah, wah, wah, *wah*. The room begins to go around. It is almost better than alcohol, this sacred loopiness. The release and deliverance. Victor tokes up with an intense expression on his face, then gets up off the bed and begins to walk around Mallory.

"I see you," he says. "I can see you in there. Don't think you can hide from me."

Mallory is white with fear, her insides beginning to churn. A long torturous stomach-growl from a whole day of hunger escapes from her gut.

"I can hear it," Victor says, stalking around Mallory's chair. Mallory wishes her insides would shut up. "You know you're coming out of there. You know you can't stay in there forever."

Mallory begins to see vague shapes in the thick air of Victor's room.

"Ha! I saw it. It just jumped out of you," he says, truly excited. "I saw it leap into the air."

Mallory feels sick, but wants to get rid of the demon or whatever it is that makes her jab her arms, whatever it is that makes kids jeer at her whenever she walks down the street.

"Get out of my sister!" Victor roars. Mallory flinches.

"I've seen her. Shoshonee. An old, old woman with wrinkles. A witch. She's in there. She's in there."

"Get her *out!*" Mallory shrieks, blood pounding in her head.

"I have to talk to her first. Speak! Tell me why you're in my sister!"

"I want her out of me, *now.*"

"It's not that simple. I have to engage with her first. She has to recognize me, see me for what I am."

"Which is *what?*"

"It's all about power. I have to get the upper hand. Speak!"

"This is just crap," Mallory says, weeping.

"You have to believe," Victor says sharply. "In the name of the Father, and of the Son, and of the Holy Ghost, I command you, Spirit . . . "

"You don't know what you're doing," Mallory blubbers.

"Don't you want to get rid of this thing?" Victor has that look on, the one he has had so many times before. His dark brown eyes look silver. Mallory only knows that she cannot go where he is. She drags herself out of the chair and stumbles out of his room and across the hall into her bedroom, slamming the door. Grabs a pair of scissors, the ones she used to cut up the paper dolls Mum made her play with when she was eight years old, lopping off their arms and legs and heads. Rolls up the thin sleeve of her black turtleneck and draws the blade over the flesh, pressing down hard until dark gems of blood well and spill over and the pain and rage slowly escape from her body like steam from an overheated boiler.

I think I will go to the dance on Saturday anyway. I have to try. Maybe Bruce will be there. I know he will never look at me in a million billion billion years. I have a dress I can wear. Sort of short. They *can't* use those names on me in a dress. Can they?

Are you a boy or a girl? *Sucky of the world.* These are the salutations people greet me with every day of my life. Then the guidance counsellor tells me I might be just a little bit depressed because I don't have a boyfriend.

I won a poetry award, big fat hairy deal, it'll only make me even more unpopular. The poem is called "Delivery," one of my better ones, I think. It has a few good lines in it anyway:

this is a strange
horse I ride, feet
pointing up, all bloodless and blue
on a long trail of ether.

My brain swims in a vault of chrome
through the removed murmur of voices
and a distant
clinical clanking.

It won second place in a competition that was Canada-wide. The comments at the bottom were the usual thing I get from literary mags, indicating that they don't know what the hell I am talking about. "Very unique imagery! Very original work. But such dark images for such a young writer!" I guess because I am a teenage girl, my life is supposed to be one endless laugh riot, and if it isn't, it's my own goddamn fault.

I am using this new toothpaste that is supposed to whiten my teeth, also growing my hair a little longer, though all the boys have long hair now too.

Dad told me to shut up. Not for the first time. He wants me to read a book called *Psychocybernetics*, which he leaves at the bottom of the stairs all the time. Hoping I'll pick it up. Well, he used to. Yesterday it was on the stair landing all right, as usual, but in slightly different form. All ripped up into little tiny pieces in a pile. Probably what he wanted to do to me.

Anyway, I was crying and couldn't stop this time at all and Mum was ignoring me as usual and all of a sudden Dad's head appeared in the door and he was bellowing "STOP CRYING!" It worked, for a moment anyway, as I was so shit-scared I couldn't even get my breath.

The guidance counsellor thinks I am a very bright young lady but not very motivated, and could I think just a little bit more about the clothes I wear each day? So he's noticed the black, which does show dandruff, I will admit. But everything goes with everything. There are advantages.

The dress I will wear to the dance if I don't chicken out and stay home and watch *Star Trek* instead is brown and it's short and hippie-looking. It's called a dashiki, and I don't know what they'll call me when I show up in it on Saturday, but I'm going to go. The guidance counsellor says I have to try a little bit harder, also that my parents are very nice folks, strong members of the community, and I should try to be just a little bit more appreciative of all that they are doing for me.

He had a little bit of spinach or something in his front tooth the whole time, so I had something on him after all. He didn't even know. Then I sat there and imagined him fucking his wife. I've seen her. She's sexless and pink and pale with stubbly gooseflesh arms and whitish eyes with no eyelashes. Probably doesn't even know what an orgasm is. I do, in fact some days I think maybe I invented them or something and they are the best thing in the whole world, but unknown. Maybe they are too good for the masses, or I just have better ones than they do.

I will never forget the first one of all, God it must have been two whole years ago now. I was sleeping in the den on the pull-out bed because I wanted to watch a late movie. It was *On the Waterfront* with Marlon Brando and Eva Marie Saint, and Brando played Terry Malloy, this washed-up prizefighter, seemingly dumb but with this really tender, sweet side, and Eva Marie Saint played Edie Doyle, who seemed sweet but was really quite tough, a lot tougher than Terry. The two fell into this agonizing love that there was no room for in their world, and at one point Edie just put her hand on Terry's face and he looked baffled by his own heart, all that was surging up inside of him. Then Edie puts her dead brother's jacket over Terry to keep him warm, and this incredible music by Leonard Bernstein just swells and swells and swells, and something is happening inside me as well but I can barely comprehend what it is. I watch the whole long movie with this feeling swelling and fizzing inside of me and then I am putting my hand down there where it has gone so many times before, but it's as if this time I know what to do and I do it and do it and do it and ... *man.* A feeling comes, a great warm bulging glowing ball of feeling that swells and swells and swells and feels as if it must *pop*—like something ripe that can't stop itself from bursting open, like some seed pod groaning on the verge of explosion—and when it does, all is glory glory *glory* and I am crying even though I have never felt so incredibly good in my life and I am not one tiny little bit sad at all.

Terry.

I am in love with Terry and must find out everything I can about Marlon Brando at the library, except that the stuff I'm finding out really isn't very appealing at all. He's old, for one thing, like over forty now, and sort of fat and likes these Tahitian women and fathers kids all over the place like puppies.

So how could he make me feel like that? How could he take my body and my soul to such ravishing heights? How could I feel so in touch with the glowing core of his very being?

Must be some kind of magic.

MR. LIVINGSTON

Mallory loathes school, the wretched swamp of the endless, ass-dragging day crushing the life out of her five days a week. But there is one tiny bright spot in the wasteland: Mr. Livingston, her English teacher, who almost seems to have a couple of brain cells to rub together, unlike most of the teachers at Kennewick High, who are so *thick* they make Mallory want to scream with frustration and despair.

Mr. Livingston wanted to be a writer, Mallory has already figured that much out. He didn't even have to say. He gives a talk one morning on a poem out of their new textbook, *Poetry of Relevance*, an attempt to force the bitter medicine of William Blake and John Keats down their unsuspecting throats with little sugar-coated doses of Joni Mitchell, Jim Morrison and John Lennon. Only this is a really good poem for once, all about Hiroshima and people disappearing when the bomb went off, just turning to vapour, and there's a certain light in Mr. Livingston's eyes when he talks about this poem, about old Mr. Ekahomo striking a match to light his pipe and the whole world catching and dissolving in flame. And that certain light in Mr. Livingston's eyes seems to meet and match a certain light in Mallory Mardling's eyes, for though she tries to hide it because it is the least cool thing in the entire world, Mallory loves loves *loves* English literature and poetry with her whole being, and wants to be a writer more than anything else in the world.

So while Mr. Livingston talks about this Hiroshima poem, a certain bright subtle thread of connection is made, or is she only imagining it? It's hard to say, for he tries to distribute his gaze evenly to all the other bored, zoned-out kids with their big feet thrust out into the aisles and drool running down their faces. Play to the crowd, that's it, even though only one kid in this room is even remotely capable of knowing what the hell you are talking about, and we all know who that is, it's the fucking freak over here, the freak who loves English literature more than life itself and yearns to be a real writer with books out, the kind of writer who moves people and wins awards, the Nobel Prize maybe, or at least a Governor General award.

This slim bright thread of connection, undeveloped, maybe not even really there, somehow sustains Mallory sufficiently to keep her from taking all her mum's Librium pills at once, even though some days she really wants to, just wants out of this whole sick rotten boring depressing deal forever. Mr. Livingston has no idea, but his little talks on poetry are sustaining a human life. Mallory wonders if anyone else has any idea how powerful words can be. Probably not. So it will remain her little secret, quite possibly for the rest of her life.

THE CLUB

At first, Mallory is surprised to be included in anything at all.

She has been shoved to the outer limits since "The Farmer in the Dell" and has become so accustomed to it, the thought of being part of any kind of social interaction is completely foreign.

But there are some weird kids hanging out now at Kennewick High. "Freaks." They look different, they dress different, and not all of them are attractive. To Mallory, this is a plus.

They smell like hash, which is a familiar smell. They know all the Dylan lyrics, like "Gates of Eden" and "It's All Right, Ma" and "Subterranean Homesick Blues." Mallory didn't think anyone else knew all the Dylan lyrics, except her and Victor, who's locked up somewhere now anyway, in some place in Toronto she's not allowed to visit.

So one day one of the girls, Gail, comes to talk to her. This happens at lunch. No one, but no one, will be seen having lunch with Mallory Mardling. This big tough-looking girl, who must weigh close to two hundred pounds, sits down next to her in the cafeteria and scares her half to death.

"I've seen you walking," she says to Mallory.

"What?"

"Walking by yourself. How come you're always alone?"

"I don't know."

"I've seen you writing under your desk."

"Is that any of your business?"

"It's poetry, isn't it? Look. I do shit too, when I'm not supposed to." The big girl with the long straight hair and round gold glasses pulls out a whole bunch of papers from her bookbag.

They are pen and ink drawings of eagles, dragons, horses with wings.

"These aren't bad," Mallory says coolly, flipping through them with all the calm detachment of an art critic.

"I'm going to be an illustrator. Or else a cartoonist, like R. Crumb."

"You mean, the guy who does Fritz the Cat?"

"That's the one. They say chicks can't do stuff like that. Bullshit. Do you have a boyfriend?"

"Ummm, not at the moment." Mallory thinks of Marlon Brando in *On the Waterfront*. "I'm sort of between boyfriends right now."

"You should come over."

"Come over?"

"It'd be cool. My parents are never around. They're divorced. I sort of stay with my aunt. She's crazy, but I like her. You'd like her too. Her name is Harriet."

"Ummmm . . ." Mallory's head is whirling. There must be some kind of mistake here, because this feels like an invitation. She doesn't like this girl particularly, but suddenly finds she wants to pounce on her offer like a starving dog.

"Friday night, eh? Three-thirty-three Tamarack Place. It's got a trailer parked out front. My Aunt Harriet's boyfriend Dominic sort of lives there." Mallory pictures one of those front yards with rusted metal, doll heads and wrecked baby carriages strewn all over the lawn. She feels repelled.

"Okay, I'll come."

"Got any shit?"

Shit. It takes Mallory a minute to figure out what it means.

"Oh. No. My brother used to . . . I mean, I don't know where he used to get it. But he's in the hospital now."

"The hospital? What'd he do, try to off himself?"

It's true, but Mallory isn't about to admit it.

"He's in the Clarke Institute."

"Oh, far out, man, the loony bin! Is he a schizophrenic or something?"

"Schizo-affective disorder."

"So he used to score dope?"

"I guess so. I could look in his room. He might've left something behind. Besides Pixy Stix, I mean."

"Bring the Pixy Stix. We get the munchies."

"We?"

"It's a club, sort of."

"Are you sure about this?" Mallory is still convinced there's been a mistake.

"Look, some of us have been talking about you. Somebody broke into the file cabinet and pulled out all your old school records. Your IQ is one hundred and fifty-two fucking points. That's enough to give you a nosebleed. And Cal saw one of your poems."

Oh my God.

"He looked over your shoulder. Says you were in some sort of a freaking trance and didn't even notice him. But he says it was pretty good shit."

Cal is this hippie-looking guy, very cute but freaky, with pinwheel eyes that never seem to be looking at you straight.

"I'm not sure my mum is going to go for this."

"Fuck your parents. Do you really think they give a shit about what happens to you?"

"I know they don't." After she has said it, Mallory realizes with a shock that it's true.

"Then come on over. Bring your jammies. Tell your mum it's a sleepover with a bunch of girls. She doesn't have to know."

"She'll never believe me."

"Hey, man. You got no social life, right? That freaks parents right out. This'll give her some hope."

Mallory sits there for a moment, a little stunned. She looks into the big girl's eyes, notices her pupils are dilated. Is she stoned, or could it be something else? Mallory feels warmed by the attention. Someone sees her, actually sees her. She catches a tiny reflection of herself in their shiny black surface.

Then, slowly, a subversive, foxy smile spreads itself over her small white face. Transformed by the potent drug of acceptance, for one heartbreaking moment Mallory looks dazzlingly, almost frighteningly attractive.

FIRST NIGHT

Mallory packs everything carefully, including the hash and the Pixy Stix. She finds a copy of *Beautiful Losers* in Victor's room, with lots of passages in it underlined with a black felt pen. She doesn't have decent pyjamas and has a moment of agonized indecision over the marks on her arms. The latest is a partly healed cigarette burn she keeps picking at. Then she decides that with kids like this, marks on your arms are probably considered a badge of honour.

She's right. Cal, who is very cute but needs a bath pretty badly, has given himself homemade tattoos with a ballpoint pen forced under the skin. Gail, the fat girl she talked to in the cafeteria, pierced her own ears with a darning needle. She thinks they were on a wavelength while they were talking at lunch and wants to initiate Mallory into the Club.

First there is the vodka. Mallory's no stranger to the stuff because she sneaks snorts out of her father's liquor cabinet fairly frequently. So she passes this test with flying colours and even garners applause. Mallory believes that next to touching her hot button and detonating the primal explosion, being drunk is very likely the best feeling there is in the whole freaking world.

Then there is the dope, no challenge. Mallory is already a pro. That old familiar wheeeee! feeling sings between her ears, and now even stinky Cal is starting to look pretty good. She wants to share something with the group but doesn't dare read the reams of poetry she has brought along in her overnight bag. These aren't the Bruce poems, they sucked anyway, she wrote those with her hormones instead of her brain, but the good ones, the ones that are starting to win awards. So she pulls out *Beautiful Losers*, Leonard Cohen's paean to the obscure Native saint Kateri

Tetakwitha, and begins to read a long passage, one of Mallory's favourites, reverberating with grief and longing. But nobody seems interested in Cohen's achingly beautiful prose poem. All they want to hear is the sex stuff with F., that scene in the car where he masturbates and comes all over the dashboard, the heroin scene, or maybe the part where Edith is squished under the elevator car.

So they would probably think *Catcher in the Rye* is way too tame, even though Mallory thinks it's right up there with *Lord of the Flies* in telling the truth about the human race.

She reads on, determined to educate them, but can see by their bored, jaded expressions that she's losing them.

"Never mind Leonard Cohen," says Kathy, a fairly straight-looking girl glued to a fuzzy-headed freak named Brent. "We've heard all that shit before. Read us some of your own stuff."

"Yeah. C'mon, Mallory. We know you write them under your desk."

"C'mon, bitch. Let's hear it!"

Mallory feels like a celebrity.

She ducks her head, blushing, and rummages in the overnight bag. Under the bottles of Acnomel and the Cover Girl pancake makeup are sheafs of things she's written, much of it in the past few weeks, and never shown to anyone. Too painful.

She does not know where to start. Read the one that won the award? But it isn't a personal favourite. How about this one? It's not very good, in fact it nearly went into the fireplace with the Bruce poems. But it's a little more . . . accessible.

"You walked into my dream, and left your footprints on my skin
I couldn't tell if loving you was joy or sin
It seems that when I touch you, I fall right in
And so, I stay away."

"Hey, Mallory, that sounds like a song."
"Sing it, Mal!"

"C'mon, bitch, sing it!"

Mallory is laughing. They're right, it does sound like a song lyric. It's not bad. Not bad at all.

So she starts singing the poem, just making the tune up on the spot, like a jazz thing, and it feels exhilarating, her head is humming with new-found power: "You stole my joy, you silly, silly boy . . . "

"All right," says Cal, and somehow his approval is the sweetest of all.

"You're better than Joni Mitchell," says this other kid, up to now a quiet kid, whose name Mallory can't remember.

Emboldened, she pulls out a real poem this time, the one she wrote after watching *The Wizard of Oz* for the fourteenth time on TV, except that she knows the poem isn't about a tin woodman at all, it's about Mr. Livingston.

She begins to read:

"TIN MAN
He walks through
robot days,
listening to the echo in his chest.

Quicksilver tears
spill from his liquid eyebeams
to fuse his jaws in place

And then one night it rains.

Waiting
for the tender mercy of an oilcan
he holds his rusted axe aloft,

Frozen in mid-chop."

Brent looks at Kathy, his eyes wide with amazement. "Shit, this kid's a genius."

"Yeah, she is," says Gail. "Her IQ is one hundred and fifty-two fucking points."

"Hey, that's as high as Pierre fucking Trudeau."

But there is another part of the initiation coming, and Mallory can feel it.

She can feel it before anyone says anything, the way you can tell something creepy is going to happen in a novel or a film.

"Right," Cal says, sucking the last bit of sweetness out of a roach. "So who's gonna do the honours?"

A snigger goes around the room. There's an awkward silence.

"I want to," says Gail.

"Oh God no," groans a guy curled up in the corner who looks like a reptile.

"Simon, relax. She's ... you know. She's like me."

"How can you tell? I mean, she's a little flat and all ... "

"I think she's cute. She looks like a boy."

At this Mallory flinches. But it is hardly anything new. And at least no one has called her manwoman.

Not so far.

"Can I go first?"

"Simon the fucker." Gail drags on her Camel, then stubs it out. "Loves to deflower the maidens."

But Simon is even scarier than the rest of them. He's six and a half feet tall, for one thing, long and lean and flexible like a snake, and so intense it looks like he's going to burst right out of his shiny skin. Real tattoos squirm on his upper arms, skulls and coffins and things. He's missing a chip off his front tooth. Mallory is afraid this is going to hurt.

"I'd rather be with Gail," she says softly, although she hardly knows what she is saying.

Gail is over the moon. She almost bodily drags Mallory into the bedroom, closes the door and starts undressing her. Without the dope in her head Mallory would probably find this completely humiliating, but with the dope in her head it is almost a pleasure. Soon she is standing naked, covered in gooseflesh even though it's warm for April, her nipples erect, with no idea of what will happen to her next.

Then Gail begins to undress, and Mallory realizes she has made a mistake. In fact, Mallory discovers in that moment that she isn't a queer at all and never will be, because the sight of Gail's pale flabby body makes her almost physically sick. It's like watching her mother undress, almost obscene. But it seems too late to turn back now.

"Now, my lovely," says Gail, and wraps her fat arms around Mallory. Mallory turns completely cold. All the pleasure has seeped away.

"I don't think I like girls," she says in a small voice, and Gail looks angry.

"How do you know? You're a virgin, right?"

"It's nothing personal."

"Just try it. Relax. It'll feel beautiful."

But it doesn't feel beautiful. It merely feels weird when Gail begins to kiss her all down the length of her pale narrow body. This is nothing like *On the Waterfront*, or the Bob Dylan backstage fantasy, or even the one where she is nude and riding a horse.

Gail kisses down and down and down, and her kisses are kind of slobbery and wet and when she gets to the modest bush of black hair at the base of her pelvis, she says, "Spread your legs."

"I'm not sure I want to do this."

"You've felt yourself up, right?"

"Right."

"This will be even better."

Gail delicately parts the dark pink labia with her tongue and pulls back to have a look.

"My . . . *God*."

"What's the matter?"

"Oh, my . . . God! It's the size of an *egg!*"

"Fuck off." Mallory slams her legs shut, humiliated by the subversive burn of pleasure that cracks through her disgust.

"I've never seen one that big."

"It's just a clit. *You* should know what they look like."

"Yeah, but it looks almost like a ..."

Mallory has started to cry now and can't stop. She grabs her clothes and starts to jam them back on her body, frantic for protection.

All of a sudden Gail seems to feel bad. "I'm sorry, sweetie, it's just that ..."

"So I don't look like you. Why do you think they call me man-woman?"

"I never meant to hurt your feelings." Gail looks genuinely remorseful.

"So what happens now? Am I out of the Club?"

"Of course not. I'll just tell them I made you come. They never need to know."

"Thanks. I think."

"Mallory, maybe you're just not the kind of girl who likes sex."

"Are you kidding? I can't keep my hands off myself. I think it must be a disease."

"No, I mean the other kind of sex. With a ... partner."

"How am I supposed to know?"

"Sex with boys is really disgusting. They always put it in too fast, for one thing. My Aunt Harriet's boyfriend Dominic ... well." Gail looks away.

"Maybe it's not so disgusting if you like the boy."

"I wouldn't know. I hate 'em." Gail is sitting on the edge of the bed with one beefy leg drawn up, so that Mallory can see her genitals. Suddenly she feels completely lucid; the stone is gone and it's depressing.

"Maybe I'm a little young."

"I was eleven. You're what, fourteen?"

"I sort of like Cal."

"You're kidding! Yeah, he's cute, all right. He has a nice smile. Nice eyes. But he stinks!"

"But if he bathed, I mean."

They both giggle.

Gail says in a heavy, teasing voice, "Maybe you can get into the tub with him."

"Yeah, with a rubber duckie."

"It might be fun to wash him you-know-where. Haven't you ever wanted to play with one?"

"I've been curious."

"If I had one, I'd be playing with it all the time."

"I guess I would too. It's just so obvious, sticking out like that . . . "

"Guys get hard at the drop of a hat."

"I thought you didn't like them. Boys, I mean."

"Oh well. I've had it both ways. C'mon, sweetie. You can join the group now."

"So I passed the test?"

"Hey, don't worry. I heard your poetry. You're in. Even with a clit like a doorknob."

At this, Mallory can't help but smile.

VICTOR, OUT OF THE HOSPITAL

It's weird at home, even weirder than usual. Mallory's big sister Nola is being a real bitch and her first-born sense of entitlement is galling.

"Your whole room stinks," Nola says to her one morning as Mallory's getting ready for another dreary, endless day at school.

"It doesn't stink."

"You been smoking pot in here?" She waves her bedroom slipper in front of her face. She's nineteen but looks puffy and middle-aged, her head wrapped in an old pink towel with holes in it.

"It's incense."

"You can get high on incense."

I wish, Mallory thinks.

"Those kids you've been hanging out with. They're the dregs of society, don't you know that? Mum's going to have a fit when she finds out."

"It's none of Mum's business."

"Yeah, well, she'll make it her business."

"You won't tell?"

"I'm not a snitch." Nola turns disdainfully on her bedroom-slippered heel and exits.

The room does smell. It smells like stale potato chips, old sheets that haven't been changed in a long time, tear-soaked pillowcases, dead flowers, ashes, banana peels, vanilla-scented Windsong perfume and shoes.

Mallory doesn't go over to Victor's room across the hall any more. She is a little scared of Victor now. There is a blank space where his brain used to be. Something happened when he went away to university. Took some funny pills or something, and then

38

they found him standing at a busy intersection at rush hour, trying to direct traffic with his thoughts.

Victor barely talks now. He mumbles, and what he says doesn't make much sense, except to him. His walk is a flat-footed psychward shuffle, and there is something odd and removed about his eyes. They seem to see in, not out. He's on something called "major tranks" and massive doses of niacinamide. It's an experimental treatment for schizophrenia that does not seem to be doing any good. And he smells rank and strange, plasticine mixed with animal cage, the smell of imbalance. Mallory misses the old Victor, but not as much as she thought she would. It's all because of the Club. She spends as much time as she can over at Gail's house, and, yes, her mother is pleased, really pleased that Mallory has a social group at last. She'll never be as popular as Nola, but never mind. And maybe soon she'll have a boyfriend, someone to hold hands with, go to the movies with, dispelling the secret terror that her boy-looking daughter might be queer.

Mallory wants a boyfriend, all right. Sometimes she wonders how she will live another day without touching one. She wants to slowly undress Cal, one item of clothing at a time, start at the top of his head and kiss down every square inch of him, not stopping until she is kissing his cock. That is not the sort of scenario Mrs. Mardling has in mind, no, not at all.

Mallory is a genius. She thinks of the perfect way to make her new social group appear acceptable to her mum. She invites Kathy, the straightest-looking girl in the Club, over for supper one night.

The only odd thing is that Kathy doesn't eat meat, but Mum seems willing to let this go by. She's probably on some sort of diet to keep her figure trim. Kathy is a smart kid, knowing instinctively what to say to keep her parents happy, manipulating them beautifully without their awareness. Though she lives in the land of freaks, she slips easily into the straight realm, working both sides of the street with alacrity, slipping from world to world in a way that will win her future prizes in a life exquisitely devoted to corporate crime. But all that is still ahead of her now.

She chats brightly with Mum, appearing to be a total extrovert, though Mallory thinks that deep down she is just as paralytically shy as she is. *God, she's good,* Mallory thinks, taking mental notes on the smooth, almost graceful way Kathy operates, dishing up total bullshit while seeming sincere. This is a much better way to maintain a cover than always wearing black or covering up your arms.

Mallory sees Cal often, doesn't talk to him, but lusts for him nonetheless. If anyone had any idea of the intensity of a young adolescent girl's sexual desire for a boy, they would run the other way. He smells, but somehow his gaminess only adds to his charm. Mallory wants to ravage him, to take him to her bed and show him what she is made of, but instead stars him in yet another poetry cycle in which he is known as the Wizard of Words.

Someone points out to her that this phrase shows up in an Alpha-Bits commercial, and in abject humiliation she burns all the poems in the fireplace, weeping with dismay. Then she writes some more.

Poetry is her wild horse, and it will not stop running.

CUNT

Mallory does not know how powerful the Club is until one Wednesday afternoon in school.

Walking to physics class, Mallory sees someone coming. Bearing down on her, to be more accurate. One of the popular kids. Acceptable kids, is more like it—no one likes her very much, but because her father is assistant principal at Kennewick High, she has a certain you-can't-touch-me cachet.

Her name is Laura Cunningham and she has longish ginger hair and dresses very primly in short, plaid pleated skirts that make her look sort of like a Catholic schoolgirl.

She sweeps up to Mallory and runs her amber-coloured eyes over her like a search beam.

"Cunt."

Mallory is used to this, and the Novocaine of throttled emotion fills her almost immediately with a welcome deadness.

But this time it's different.

Snake-eyes Simon hears what Laura calls her.

Simon says nothing. Merely files it away. And later that afternoon when school is out, Laura Cunningham, walking home, is surrounded by a cadre of five kids.

The five kids walk her into a secluded area behind the school.

First they only talk to her.

She doesn't respond well.

It takes two of them to hold her down.

They use a stick. That way they can't be charged with anything too specific.

The weird thing, and the saving thing, is that these five kids aren't from the school. They aren't even from the Club. No one has ever seen them before and no one will ever see them again.

41

And Laura Cunningham does not tell.

She's an acceptable kid, but not that acceptable. She doesn't have that much to trade on.

And she's ashamed.

Mallory will not be called "cunt" in public again.

MALLORY, WITH HORSES

There is a way to get through childhood, the aridity, the isolation, the shame.

Mallory is eleven. If she could have a horse, everything would be different.

Annie Voortman next door would stop tormenting her. Annie would be envious. Annie would be forever trying to get on her good side, instead of the other way around.

If Mallory had a horse, she would name him Silvernor and he would be an Arab. She would ride him beside the railroad tracks out Beaverton Road, fleet as lightning.

Nola would leave her alone. Nola might want to ride Silvernor, but Mallory would not allow it.

Silvernor is *her* horse.

All of Mallory's childhood, it seems, is a "then it would be," with almost none of it actual. She is like a tree growing out of solid rock, barely nourished, yet surviving on whatever minerals she can suck out of sheer granite.

One thing is real: the taunting, the kicking, the manwoman. Mallory is about to erupt into puberty, and it is as if the kids can smell it on her, as it's escalating, getting worse.

Mallory's horse is a horse of the mind, a horse with more potency than any horse who ever actually lived. Mallory does not realize that the horse is just an extension of her own energy and that eventually, only a few years away, though it will seem more like a hundred, that horse will take the bit between his ferocious teeth and charge.

It is all beginning to happen, right now.

THE ESSAY

Mr. Livingston in English class is beginning to take notice of Mallory.

It's not as if he has never noticed her before. But there is something disturbing about the girl. The way she ducks her head, as if not to be seen. The strange garb. The haunted intelligence in her eyes, which Mr. Livingston has always found off-putting.

When a student's IQ level is some thirty-five points higher than the teacher's, then there is a problem. Such a problem began to be evident back in grade school, when Mallory was put on an accelerated track of taking two grades in one to prepare her for a special gifted class in grade five.

This was a social and educational experiment in which thirty-two children with intelligence levels in the exceptional range were bussed in from all over the district and crammed into one classroom together. They called it the Major Work Class, though normal kids in the screeching, snake-ridden Amazon of the playground dubbed them the Brains.

To be a Brain was the worst thing you could be, but at least there was strength in numbers. The school board made the brilliant decision to hire Mr. Service, fresh-faced and earnest, a complete greenhorn straight out of teacher's college. By mid-year, the manipulative little freaks of the Major Work Class had reduced him to rubble, and he had to be hospitalized for several weeks due to "nervous exhaustion."

An aura of triumph glowed in the classroom in his absence. When Mr. Service returned, he was an ashen, reduced version of himself. He limped along in the school system for two more years, then, dripping with shame, slunk away into self-imposed exile as an insurance salesman.

Such is the strange, corrosive power of high intelligence, and the way it can reduce the less brilliant bulbs in the box to powder in frighteningly short order.

Mallory has some idea of her power, but she hates it. She remembers trying to explain to Mr. Service how she was able to make a book report deadline in the space of three hours, even though she hadn't even cracked the book: she read *Huckleberry Finn* using her special technique of running her eye down the page *(doesn't everyone know how to do this?)*, scooping up the gist of the information in a few seconds, a form of speed-reading she had always used in school and took completely for granted.

Mr. Service looked at her in bafflement and shook his head: *no, Mallory, no one can read that fast, it simply isn't possible*. Reluctantly, she agreed; *oh, okay, then I didn't*. It was easier that way. But her report on *Huckleberry Finn* still earned her an A-plus.

So teacherly misunderstanding is nothing new to her. Mr. Livingston so obviously does not get her poems that she no longer even hands them in. He sent the first one back riddled with question marks: "What is this—???" Mallory is using vocabulary that Mr. Livingston isn't familiar with. She includes the word "gelid" in one verse ("green fish suspended/in gelid waters/under the glittering crust of the lake"), and he crosses it out with the notation "No such word." Her verbal audacity at such a young age frightens him a little, so he chastises her with red ink. She is such a strange little girl. No fingernails at all. Perhaps suffering from a personality disorder—he must ask the guidance counsellor, Mr. Crofton, to pull her file for him. He secretly enjoys pulling the files of children who are marginalized by some psychosocial disability. Intelligence is a new one, however, and perhaps more intimidating than bed wetting, masturbation, a career mother or a father who secretly drinks.

But then! Mallory gets a surprise one day, an extremely high mark on her English Comp assignment, an A-plus. It makes her catch her breath. She garners mostly Bs and B-pluses, marks invariably taken off due to all the red question marks, the "does not follow" or "where are you going with this?" in the margins.

She shows Gail.

"Far out," says Gail, not really interested. Five of them are sitting in the corner of the cafeteria, planning to score some dope for the weekend.

"But this is significant. Mr. Livingston never gets my stuff."

"That's because he's a dickhead."

Then they go on to other matters. Mallory is a little disappointed in their mild reaction to what seems to her like a clear victory. A battle at least partially won.

The essay, entitled "The Rebirth of Wonder: Contemporary Images and Social Commentary in Lawrence Ferlinghetti's *I Am Waiting*," will be published in the Kennewick High yearbook at the end of the school year, but by the time the brand-spanking-new copies of *The Wick* are handed out to all the eager young students, Mallory will have disappeared.

"Oh, Mallory," says Mr. Livingston casually as she prepares to bolt out the door for a smoke in the courtyard after another interminable lecture on bad poetry.

She looks up incredulously, her face a study in "you mean *me?*" He nods.

She freezes.

What does he want?

Today's poem was an abomination called "The Glory of Work" by Abigail Curran, and it is perhaps the worst piece of tripe Mallory has ever heard. She feels actual nausea when Mr. Livingston reads it in a pretentious, actorish voice that only inflates the pompous doggerel to Hindenburgesque proportions:

"O what immortal passion, surging fierce within the soul
Can seize the mind like daily work:
The rapt'rous, shining goal!"

Freudian sublimation horseshit, thinks Mallory.

"For Work is God's own glory, bending purpose to His will,
Its channelled ardour speeds the blood
In grand, exalted thrill."

Mallory thinks Mr. Livingston secretly beats off to this stuff, his teacherly heart all afire. Abigail Curran was probably some dried-up old spinster who lived a hundred years ago and never saw any action in her entire life. The subtext of squirming sexuality gives Mallory the creeps.

"What are the primary images in this poem? Class?"

The question falls flat.

"Anybody?"

Numb silence.

"How about the horses? You know, the snorting steeds being reined back in the third stanza. What do they represent?"

Mr. Livingston appears to be completely unaware of the huge, invisible WHO CARES? sign suspended above the kids' nodding heads. Mallory's blood has congealed into a semi-solid by the time she bolts for the door. Mr. Livingston's summons is like a tripwire, but she also feels a little intrigued. What could he possibly want with her?

Then her gut lurches. *No, it can't be.*

But she meekly stands before him, curiosity overcoming dread.

"Mallory, I've been noticing an improvement in the quality of your assignments lately," he begins, eyeing her up and down.

The last student files out of the classroom. Mr. Livingston pushes the door closed with his foot.

"Uh . . . thank you, sir."

"You're quite a talented young lady. I heard about the poetry award."

"It was second place."

He looks confused, then laughs, turning a little red.

"You only aim for the top, eh, Mallory?"

"I guess so."

"I've noticed you're . . . coming out of yourself a little bit more lately. Talking to the other kids. That's good."

She tilts her head a little and looks at him. His heart begins to beat a bit faster. He notices for the first time that her eyes are crystalline blue and grey, almost like the eyes of a wild creature, perhaps a wolf. Fascinating.

"But the thing is, Mallory, I've noticed that the kids you're hanging around with are . . . well, let's just say these are kids who have some problems."

Simon with his jackknife, Gail seducing girls, Kathy stealing cosmetics from the Rexall store . . .

"And your point?" Mallory can't believe she is saying this, but it comes out of her mouth anyway.

Miraculously, she gets away with it.

Then she feels something.

Something she does not want to feel.

Body heat.

Heat that is coming from Mr. Livingston's body. And a smell, like overheated deodorant and fried aftershave, the alcohol-laced Aqua Velva odour she knows well from taking a swig out of her father's bottle.

Her body begins to respond, though it is the last thing on earth that she wants.

He fixes her with his gaze. His eyes are brown and kindly, but the pupils are dilated.

"Mallory, I think you need just a little bit of guidance at this juncture. If you took a wrong direction at this point in your life, it could have serious repercussions."

He's turned on. That's what it is. Mallory sees it. Sees in her peripheral vision (because, like a solar eclipse, she dares not look straight at it) the burgeoning erection in his tweedy baggy teacherly pants. She is both repulsed and enthralled. Wants to run and wants equally to stay. Wants to further explore this strange new power she seems to have, the power to affect someone else's body.

"I'd like to take you under my wing."

I'll bet you would, thinks Mallory.

"Children like you, gifted children, need some special support. Someone to help them develop their gifts. I'd like to see you blossom, Mallory. You have tremendous potential. Right now you're shy, but believe me, with the right sort of encouragement, you could flower into an exceptionally attractive young lady. I can see signs of it in you already."

Mallory is slowly being sucked into the seductive trap of being special. It is a candy impossible to resist.

He reaches out and brushes a stray lock of her dark hair back from her forehead. This triggers in her young pelvis an energy zoom of exhilarating intensity.

"I'd like to spend some time with you after class. Just talking. Maybe you can show me more of your poems. I can help you develop them, Mallory. I did some dabbling in poetry myself, in college. I can show you how to make them more accessible to readers."

Mallory tenses, her mind turning over. *Shit. If he touches my poems, he's dead.*

And yet. He is a way to power.

"Perhaps what you need is a mentor, Mallory. And I'd like to be that mentor."

"Thank you, sir."

"Call me Kenneth."

"What?"

"I think if we're going to have a special relationship, we should dispense with the usual formalities and be on a first-name basis."

"Okay . . . Kenneth." Mallory wants to call him Ken or even Kenny, but does not dare. Part of her is enjoying the surrealism of the scene; the rest of her is terrified. He is now fully erect and breathing a little unsteadily. She knows she must escape, and fast, but the erection affects her like a fanned-out cobra head weaving seductively back and forth. She feels nailed to the spot.

"And Mallory."

"Yes?"

"It might be a good idea, at least for right now, if you don't tell the other kids about this. There might be some envy. You know how they can be."

"Believe me, I know," Mallory says, her face stretching into an idiot smile.

"And maybe don't share this with your folks, not just yet. That'll make it more ... special."

"Okay ... Kenneth." She can't suppress a girlish giggle.

For Mallory is fourteen, a colt. Her superheated brain is a burden, cooking her psyche and inflaming it dangerously. She is a fourteen-year-old girl among kids who are two and three years older, because she "skipped," accelerated through the primary grades quickly to prepare herself for that great educational opportunity, the Major Work Class.

She is out of her depth.

Drowning swimmers will clutch at anything. When she walks out of Kenneth's classroom, she truly does feel special, maybe for the first time in her whole life.

And it is the most intoxicating feeling in the world.

ANNIE

It's Annie who first brings the group to the Rev.

The same Annie, the one Mallory grew up with, the one with the pigeons in the backyard, the one who moved away years ago and who Mallory assumed would never show her freckly blonde face in Mallory's presence again.

Anika Voortman, the bossy big-sister figure (as if Mallory needed another one of those), even though they were the very same age.

Anika Voortman, the one who invited Mallory to her eleventh birthday party and told her she had to play a game to get any cake.

In the game, Mallory is blindfolded. She should be clued in, but, desperate to belong, isn't. So she goes along with it.

And they spin her around and around. Around and around and around, until she is dizzy and disoriented.

Then the seven girls in their prettiest dresses stand in a merry little circle all around her.

And Annie does the countdown: "Five ... four ... three ... two ... one ... "

Each of them tips back a filled pink-and-white party glass.

"Blastoff!"

And Mallory is completely saturated with warm, mucousy mouthfuls of spat-out lemonade. A hail of laughter pounds her skin. She stands in the middle of the circle of shrieking girls, blind, wet.

And goes home crying. She will never forget. She hates Annie, will hate her forever. When Annie moves away a little while later, she is glad. She does not say goodbye, although her mother nearly forces her.

"She's lived next door to you for eleven years! Your whole life,

Mallory. She used to be your best friend. You always had your birthdays together. Honestly, what is wrong with you?"

"She's mean to me."

"It's all in your imagination. You should count yourself lucky to be included in her social group. She's such an attractive girl, with that long blonde hair."

Parents live on the dark side of the moon. They have no clue, no living clue, as to what their kids are really about.

As with so many things, Mallory gets used to this, just one more of the conditions of her outworld existence, the icy wind of exile whistling through her ribs.

And so she is flabbergasted when one night Annie Voortman shows up at the Club.

She looks gorgeous, which makes it even worse. Tall, golden, slim-legged, fierce-eyed, beautiful, with all the grace, poise and vitality that Mallory lacks. She sucks it out of other people—this Mallory knows—but no one else is in on her secret.

"Hullo, Mallory."

"Annie. Fancy meeting you here."

"What's that supposed to mean?"

"I just didn't think we were your type. You know. We're all a bunch of crazy freaks."

"Speak for yourself."

"You haven't changed much."

"Neither have you. Still wearing black. But I see you got your ears pierced."

"Gail pierced them for me."

"The fat girl?"

"Gail is all right."

"You like her? Well, there's no accounting for people's tastes." She takes a long drag on her Export A.

Annie passes the initiation test easily, with Simon gladly doing the honours. But Annie has some pretty strange ideas that the Club has never encountered before.

She goes to church.

No kidding.

Some of the kids like to trade Catholic horror stories about masturbation and the jackbooted nuns at Blessed Sacrament, but this is a different kind of church, a nice white-painted middle-of-the-road church called Kennewick United.

The only reason Annie goes there at all is because of the Rev.

"You've got to meet this guy," Annie tells the group while they look at her, puzzled. "He is the coolest. He talks about the Nazz all the time."

"The Nazz?"

"Y'know. Jesus. Makes it sound so neat, as if you're there or something. And he has a group, a really cool group that meets in the church basement. You can bring a bottle or a joint if you want, so long as you're careful."

"In a United church?" Mallory is incredulous. The United church she used to go to for Sunday school was as harmless, as innocuous as a slice of white bread.

"The Rev is cool. The people in the church don't know about the group. Well, they know, but they don't understand what's really going on."

"Is that his name? I mean ... "

"His name is Dolph. Well, I call him Dolph, anyway. The Reverend Randolph Fletcher."

Now Mallory remembers. She has seen his name in the paper. And his picture: a bald head, a formidable moustache. He seemed about nine feet tall. The Reverend Randolph Fletcher is relatively new to the church and a bit of a firebrand, speaking out on social issues such as poverty and desegregation. In the article he was quoted as saying his hero and model is the late Dr. Martin Luther King, Jr. Mallory remembers when King was shot. It made her cry for days.

"He talks to us about all sorts of things. Like, sex."

"*Sex?*"

None of the kids in the Club has ever heard of a minister even mentioning sex, except to condemn it as terrible, filthy, perverted, a sin. Which you should carefully save for the love of your life, your partner in marriage.

"Is he a queer or something?"

"Don't believe the rumours. It's not true. He didn't get fired—he resigned. He was being morally persecuted in Orillia."

"Kennewick's just as boring as Orillia. Even worse, because it's smaller. He won't have any better luck here."

"You guys should come." Annie stubs out her cigarette, narrowing her exotic amber eyes at Cal, which makes Mallory seethe. "It's every Tuesday night in the basement."

"I don't think the good Reverend is going to welcome an assortment of freaks, geeks and social outcasts such as we have here," says Kathy. Mallory is starting to really like her. She's way smart, funny and sharp.

"But he's different. I'll bet you're scared to come."

"Like shit we are." Gail's back is already up.

"Maybe a couple of us can go," says Dale, one of the quieter kids.

"I think Mallory should go."

"Yeah—Mallory!" Everyone chimes in.

Once again, Mallory feels famous. "Why me?"

"Because you're our social critic. You've got the smarts to get the lay of the land, kid." Gail sounds pretty sure of herself.

Mallory thinks a minute. "Only if you'll come with me."

Gail looks at her intently. Their eyes meet.

"Okay. I will."

"Our intrepid reporters," says Cal, hugging Gail and Mallory, one in each arm. Mallory feels like she will die. She wants to melt into his arms.

No one touches Mallory. Not her parents, not her teachers, not her friends. No wonder young people make out. They're starved for contact. She has to make this fleeting touch of his last for at least a week.

And she will bring her notebook when she sees the Rev.

And a pen.

PART II:
THE REV

I haven't been inside a church in so long that it felt like a bolt of lightning was going to hit me at any minute. Hellfire and damnation. God's only function is to condemn us anyway. We don't do a good enough job on ourselves, we need God to hold the big stick over us and just wait for us to sin.

My sins include the following. Touching myself. Stealing Tanqueray gin out of the liquor cabinet. Looking in Victor's keyhole one night when I heard him beating off. Lying about the Club. Wishing Nola dead, then she got really sick with hepatitis and had to go to the hospital and I thought I made it happen. Taking a 20 out of Mum's purse, which she didn't even notice, so there were no consequences; this makes the sin worse. Wishing Dad dead the week he tore up *Psychocybernetics*. (No luck there.) Getting turned on when Mr. Livingston the creep came on to me. Coming to his office two more times and trying not to notice his hard-on as he talks to me about William Butler Yeats and the concept of radical innocence. And I'd better stop now as this list of sins is just getting too long to contemplate.

Anyway. About the church. At least it was in the basement around the back, so we didn't have to go in the, whatever-it-is, the churchy part with the stained glass, organ and pews. The *sanctuary*. So I didn't have to smell old varnish, dust, organ pipes, stale carpeting and guilt. But church basements have a smell all their own, seepy and damp and paperish, a Sunday school smell of stiff fabric and chalk and white vinyl Bibles with zippers. I couldn't believe how many kids were there—couldn't count them all. They didn't look like freaks, but then the kids in the Club don't, either, at least not all of them.

Anika was there, sitting right up at the front. She's a groupie. I can tell. Her chest was sticking way out in front of her in a tight white ⊤-shirt. Her skirt barely covered her ass.

I don't know what it is about churches that brings out such extremes in people, but these kids were really buzzed, all excited as if some rock star had come to town. I wanted to tell them—it's only a church. It's only some minister who's about to lecture us about what a bunch of sinners we are and how we're all condemned to hell unless we take a permanent vow of chastity.

And then something happened that totally changed my mind.

This guy comes out of the back room and walks up to the front, and he isn't dressed like any minister I've ever seen before, no black robe, no turned-around collar or long thingie, whatever you call that thing they wear around their necks.

He's dressed sort of ordinary but young, in chinos and a purple shirt with kind of wide sleeves. He's old, probably about 35. He looks a little bit like Gomez from *The Addams Family*, who is sort of sexy in an old kind of way, except he doesn't have much hair on top and a bristly black moustache and fiery crackly brown eyes that shine with—what? I'm still trying to figure that out.

It's hard to capture just what he said, because I think it was all in the saying. But I'll try. He's already dominating the stage like some sort of a magician, or a concert pianist. Then he starts to talk. "I can feel the energy in this room tonight," he says, pacing back and forth and smiling. "The energy you young people are generating is absolutely incredible. It's special. Because each and every one of you kids is special. Each and every one of you here tonight is a child of God. You are God's own beloved children. And with you, he is well pleased!"

This brings a huge whooping cheer like at assembly when they're giving out the awards for sports.

"When I feel energy like this burning out towards me, I have to tell you kids, I become filled with the Holy Spirit. I'm so filled with the Holy Spirit right now, I fell like I could almost explode! Did you ever have that feeling?"

" ... *Yeah!*"

"D'ye ever stop to think about where all that energy is coming from?"

" ... *Tell us!*"

"It comes from *love*. Love is what sets this place on fire. Love is what made all those amazing changes in your body that turned you from a child into a beautiful young adult. Love is the passion that makes you cry Hallelujah!"

" ... *Whoop!*"

"Love is God's sweet song to us all, the greatest gift he ever gave to humanity. The love in your hearts and your bodies is the most precious thing you will ever experience. It's natural and beautiful and 100% pure. And I feel that love so strong tonight, it's just phenomenal. It absolutely blows my mind!"

This is a mob, I'm thinking. This is *sieg heil*, the grainy footage of Nazi Germany I've seen on TV. But at the same time … it's kind of cool. He likes us. I can tell. He's not telling us what to do. He's different.

"Let's pray together right now," he says, and this isn't like any prayer I ever used to hear in church when I had to fight to try to stay awake.

"Holy God …" He reaches his arms up over his head and his face contorts like he's going to cry. "Holy Father of the Universe, source of all life, love and inspiration, *fill* this place with your presence tonight. Dear Lord, we want you to blow the roof off this house of worship with your incredible power. Let your lightning strike each and every one of these young people here with you tonight. Fill us all with the *ecstasy* of your wondrous love!"

"Oh, God!"

A shriek from the back of the room. A blandly plain, chubby blonde girl in a striped mini-dress is standing up and screaming. "Oh *God!* Oh *God!*"

"Suzie," the Rev calls out to her. "Blessed child, come up here right now and talk to me. Don't be afraid. Talk to me, dear Suzie. Tell me the secrets of your heart."

Suzie sleepwalks up to the front, tears ripping jaggedly down her fat cheeks, her eyes glazed.

"Oh God …"

"Tell us."

"It's just that the love is so *strong* …"

"It's okay, Susie, it's okay."

"I can feel it. I can feel it."

"Where can you feel it, Suzie?"

"Right here." She indicates her lower abdomen. The Rev puts his hand there, standing behind her.

Hmmm.

He begins to rub her stomach in a circle. This is weird. Suzie moans, and he prays in a deep, husky voice, "God, watch over this sweet girl, Suzie Graham. Lord, you know she's got some troubles at home. You know her parents are getting a divorce and it's just about breaking her heart." Suzie's mouth is stretched open, strings of saliva dripping. She can barely stand. The Rev is holding her up.

"Enter her body and fill her mind with your amazing presence, dear Lord."

Suzie takes in a huge, shuddering breath, and then explodes: "DADDY!"

"Let it out, Suzie," says the Rev, his own eyes misting up with tears. The crowd is cheering her on: "Way to go, Suze." "Don't be scared." "Let God love you."

"Daddy ... you betrayed me ..."

"Forgive him!" someone shouts from the crowd.

"Shhhh. Let her come to it. Let her come to it. Suzie, I know your father hurt you terribly when he had that affair with your mother's best friend. I know you didn't think you could even go on living. But here you are, Suzie. Here you are tonight. And do you know what that is? That is a miracle, Suzie. *A miracle.* God will give you the strength to get through anything. And you'll be strong, Suzie, strong for the whole family. Strong for your little brother Timmy. Strong for your mother."

At this, Suzie begins to pull herself together a bit.

"And when the time is right, God's forgiveness will enter your heart and soften it, and you'll forgive your dad the way you know you want to. All in God's good time, Suzie."

She looks at him in naked, blazing love, then throws her arms around his neck.

"I love you, Reverend Fletcher."

Pandemonium.

I can't say that I know what to make of all this. One confession led to another, and kids were standing up and saying all kinds of things. Talking about stuff they did that was wrong. About touching themselves, even, the way I do (although it was all boys). I never thought I'd hear anyone talk about that, ever. The Rev was so cool about all of it, saying God would forgive us if we could only forgive ourselves. I wonder if he's married. I didn't see a ring. I wonder if this is how he gets off.

But it was interesting. At the end of it all, I felt exhausted, and Gail and I looked at each other and went, "*Whew!*" Everyone seemed wiped out, but really eager to come back for more. And a couple of kids, Annie in particular, stayed behind in a lineup to talk to the Rev privately after the show.

Well, it felt like a show.

A blood-and-thunder show. A spectacle. But it was kind of neat. I never thought of God as the source of all that energy, what he calls love and what I'd call pure sex. I thought the two couldn't possibly be farther apart. At least that's what I was taught.

So this is getting me thinking in a whole new way. Is it worth going back? Maybe Cal would come. Probably not, though—he's such a cynic about church. But so was I. Until now.

DR. RUBENS

And then Mr. Crofton, the guidance counsellor, pronounces his verdict: he believes Mallory has some serious problems in school. Social problems.

He tells Sam and Dewla Mardling about the unsavoury characters she is spending time with at lunch hour. The giggling, the slapping, the drug jokes. The way that big girl Gail puts her arm around her. Suspicious. It seems Wilbur Crofton has been spying.

"Her English teacher, Ken Livingston, pulled her file," he tells Mrs. Mardling, who is sitting in Crofton's office, looking completely confused.

"Pulled her—what?"

"Her file, Mrs. Mardling. Ken has a few concerns about her extracurricular activities."

"Well, we're just delighted that she has a social life now. She was always so quiet," says Dewla Mardling. "Kept pretty much to herself. Couldn't get her to come out of her room. But just in the last few weeks, things started to change. She invited a girl over for supper, just a lovely girl. And she's going to church. Well, not on Sundays, but it's a youth group."

"Mrs. Mardling, we're happy to hear she's connecting with other kids. But it's the type of kid she spends time with at noon hour that has us concerned. These kids are not what you would call well adjusted."

"But what about that lovely Kathy?"

"Kathy Jamieson was suspended last year for shoplifting."

"No! I'm sure you've made a mistake."

"There's still hope for Mallory, Mrs. Mardling. She's quite intelligent, with one of the highest IQ scores in the school. In fact, only one child scored higher, and he was speaking Greek when he was five years old. Her grades in English this year are in the A-plus range. Mr. Livingston has nothing but good to say about her. We just feel she needs more intensive guidance than the school can provide. Her attitude is extremely negative and she has some strange ideas about her social orientation. She seems to feel almost persecuted."

"Why on earth would she feel like that?"

"There's a clinical term for it, Mrs. Mardling: *youth paranoia*. Most kids grow out of it once they're past that awkward stage of puberty, all those confusing changes happening in the body, the hormones and whatnot. But in her case, it's a little too severe for us to deal with here."

"Meaning?" Sam Mardling bursts in. Up until now he has kept his mouth shut, but he can't hold back a minute longer. Just what was this guy driving at? What was he trying to say about his daughter?

"Meaning that we believe she would benefit from professional help."

"She's not crazy!" booms Sam, in horror that another one of his kids will end up in the loony bin. Victor is enough of a disgrace. The excuse that he has mono is starting to wear thin.

"Mr. Mardling. Please don't misinterpret what I'm saying. We never meant to imply that your daughter is crazy. Just maladjusted. In need of intensive counselling."

So here she is.

Sitting in the waiting room.

Sweating like a horse.

A little stoned. Gail gave her a joint at lunchtime. But the stone is wearing off, and reality closing in like a hand.

Mallory can smell pot fumes streaming off her clothes, a slightly skunky reek. But she has managed to find something in her wardrobe that isn't black. The blouse is dark brown with a small white ruffle down the front. Mum bought it for her fourteenth birthday, a "girl blouse," though not girly enough that Mallory would shove it to the back of her closet. This is the first time she has ever worn it and it is a little tight across the front, because by now she has at least the beginnings of breasts. Maybe it will make her look more feminine, so the forces of normalcy will call off their dogs.

A jaundiced-looking stringbean of a guy wanders out of the inner sanctum. God, what a loser, a pock-face, typical psychiatric patient, a failure at everything. Probably couldn't get a girlfriend if he paid her with his own weekly allowance. What do you bet his name is Howie, or Hermie. How is it some males can be so incredibly sexy, and others, with all the same basic equipment, so completely repulsive?

"Miss Mardling," the brittle-looking receptionist says. "You can go in now. Dr. Rubens will be with you shortly."

Mallory wonders if he has paintings of fat women on the walls.

But: *shock*. Dr. Rubens isn't at all what she expected. For one thing, he's a woman. A wire-haired, thin-shinned, dried-out woman with some kind of vaguely Germanic accent. Ilsa, She-Devil of the SS. *Vee haf vays of making you talk.*

"Meez Mardling." She adjusts her black-framed half-glasses on a long knobbed nose, which ends in a tiny rodentlike point. Mallory takes note, so she can describe it all in her diary later. "So you haf been referred to me by Weelbur Crofton of Kennevick High."

Mallory has no idea what to say—it will all be used against her, anyway—so she only nods.

"He has passed along your file. I must say, Meez Mardling, I am impressed vith the level of your intelligence."

One hundred and fifty-two fucking IQ points, Mallory thinks. It's the only reason she was accepted into the Club: she's an intellectual freak.

"But Meester Crofton has made note of certain . . . social adjustment problems."

Here it is, then. Mallory tries to look neutral, but attentive. At this point she has nothing to say anyway. So Dr. Rubens is forced to go on.

"Extreme introversion. Zo. You are a shy gerrl, eh, Mallory?

"I guess so. People say that I am." Dr. Rubens seems to be sucking in every detail of her appearance with the twin vacuums of her eyes. Mallory crosses her arms to hide her bleedy bitten-down fingernails, but too late, the doctor has noticed them. Mallory has seen a reference to nail biting in a psychology book. It was described as "auto-cannibalism."

"Do you haf a boyfriend?"

Lie, lie, lie. "Well, yeah, sort of. I mean, there's a boy I like. His name is . . . (*Bruce Cal Mark John Mike*) Richard."

"Reechard." The sour lines in Dr. Rubens's face all curl gruesomely upward like something from an evil cartoon. "And do you and Reechard . . . "

Fuck?

"Go on dates?"

"Not exactly. We sort of . . . hang out."

"Heng . . . out?"

"Yeah. Y'know, at the park 'n stuff."

"And girlfriends?"

Mallory immediately thinks of Gail trying to seduce her at the Club.

"Yeah, I have . . . I mean, Kathy. She's my best friend." She knows Gail would feel betrayed, but Gail is fat and rough-looking and a lesbian, so not very socially desirable as a best friend.

Besides, this is survival. Gail would understand.

"Zo. Your file indicates a certain . . . social anxiety disorder. Do people make you nervous, Mallory?"

Mallory thinks: *All the time. All the time.*

"Not particularly."

"You look nervous right now."

That's because it's the Spanish Inquisition.

"Mallory, vile we are getting to know each other better, I would like to prescribe zome medication which will help ease zis anxiety you feel around other people."

"Librium?"

Dr. Rubens is taken aback. This she didn't expect.

"Why, yes."

Mallory loves Librium. She takes her mother's whenever she can get it, with a slug of Benylin cough syrup, or even a shot of her father's Old Bushmills Irish whisky from the liquor cabinet. Now she'll have a whole prescription to herself. Things are looking up.

"And Mallory. I would like to give you zome . . . homeverk. Zome little tests that will help us understand your pr-roblems." (Us? *Us*? There's no one else in the room. Mallory wonders if she'll share the test results with her husband or her lover or her girlfriend or her slave.)

The tests are something else. Several different "personality inventories," with reams and reams of strange questions. Some of them are hilarious: "Are you very afraid of black widow spiders?" "If the light bulb burned out in your bedroom, would you change it yourself or ask your father or brother to help you?" It turns out these questions are designed to indicate how masculine or feminine you are.

Mallory scores exactly down the middle.

When she comes in to see her two weeks later, Dr. Rubens shuffles through the test results, peering at them through her half-glasses with her forehead all squinched up, as if she is trying to figure out a puzzle.

"Most . . . unusual," Dr. Rubens says.

And the intelligence test. A joke. Mallory aces it, and this time scores one hundred and fifty-eight. Dr. Rubens looks at the test result, then eyes her.

"Mallory."

"Yes, Dr. Rubens."

"Vee need to be honest here. Zese test results. Are you sure you didn't ask zomeone to help you?"

"Who'd be that smart?"

This is not the answer Dr. Rubens wants to hear, at all. She writes "uncooperative" on her chart. Such a strange girl, one of the strangest she has ever treated. Dr. Rubens is formulating a diagnosis of a personality disorder with tendencies towards sexual deviancy, but wants more hard evidence to confirm her professional suspicions. She needs to know if the girl has certain habits.

"Mallory."

"Yes, Dr. Rubens."

"Haf you ever . . . explored your own body?"

"Explored?" She thinks of Jacques Cartier, Samuel Hearne, stout Cortez, doughty men whose exploits are traced on maps with red, blue and green lines.

"Touched your . . . genitalia."

"No." But she can't help but flush with shame. She masturbates practically every night, unless she has her period, and sometimes thinks people can tell just by looking at her.

"Mallory. You ken be honest vith me."

"Is that . . . bad?"

"No, no, no, of course not. It's perfectly normal. But it vould indicate . . . " Those deadly pauses. *Poison.* Dr. Rubens shuffles the papers around in Mallory's file. "Vee are concerned about your psychosexual development. About a certain lack of . . . femininity . . . in your profile, Mallory. That you may haf a tendency to be somewhat . . . "

Mallory squirms in her chair. Here it comes, here it comes . . .

"Mesculine."

So a boy can throttle his ding-dong 'til the cows come home, but she cannot touch her hot button without being labelled a queer.

"Mallory. You could improve your appearance enormously if you vere to dress a little more like a normal teenaged gerrl."

Hot pants. Ruffled peasant blouses. Low-slung, lime-green bell-bottoms. Shirts that look as if someone has thrown paint at them.

"I like black," Mallory says in a small voice.

Dr. Rubens looks at her over the swimmy thick half-glasses. The cold grey marbles of her eyes calcify.

"Black is not ze only colour."

But that's just the trouble, Mallory thinks. That's what nobody can understand.

It is.

A MOUSE WHEN IT SPINS

Victor sits in the middle of the muddle and funk of his cluttered bedroom and fiddles with string.

Victor doesn't do anything.

He stares at the wallpaper, smokes and tokes and watches *Captain Kangaroo*, just like that song that keeps coming on the radio.

Victor wastes time like nobody else on earth. Or so Sam Mardling believes. *Timewaster. Useless.* All right, we know the boy isn't well, but what about the time Dewla walked in on him trying on one of Nola's bras?

Nola is totally freaked out by this and refuses to wear it ever again, even though it was her favourite bra, a 36C black lace uplift.

"Can I have it?" Mallory asks. She has always coveted Nola's underwear.

"The pointy parts go at the front," Nola tells her, chucking the bra at her. It hits her in the face. She washes the bra over and over and puts it in a hot dryer before shoving it in her bottom drawer. Maybe she'll grow into it.

Victor wanders into the stores sometimes, and shoplifts small items like chocolate bars (Crispy Crunch) and ballpoint pens he will never use. He doesn't walk, he shambles. The shuffle isn't quite as bad as when he first came home. But he is still on major tranks, and the drugs make him strange and heavy, as if he is moving underwater or in slow motion.

It's hard for Mallory to talk to Victor at all. He's not the same. He's silly.

"Why is a mouse when it spins?" he asks her one day when she comes into his room, like old times, and sits down on the swivel chair.

"Give up?"

Mallory looks completely baffled. She gives up, all right.

"The higher the fewer." Then his face breaks into a distorted, stretched, almost leering grin.

"Remind me never to go nuts," Mallory says, pulling herself out of the swivel chair and slamming the door of his room behind her.

She feels lonely at home, but when isn't she lonely? Going to the shrink embarrasses her, but is that anything new? Mallory just gets better at telling her what she seems to want to hear: "I bought a new outfit. A short skirt and blouse. Orange paisley. I'm going to wear them to the dance on Saturday."

"Oh, goot, goot. Goot gerrl!"

The Club is a solace, a break from the grind of school, though it seems a little pointless as all they do is smoke up and listen to Dylan and Joplin and Hendrix and the Incredible String Band and slip away with whomever they happen to like that day to have sex. Mallory hasn't had sex yet, at least not with another human being, and feels an insatiable curiosity, and fear.

Four of them go to the Rev's little talks every week. Kathy and Cal are sort of going around together and they come along, holding hands continually, yelling out things like "Hallelujah!" and "Praise the name of Jesus!" Mallory is feeling more drawn in with every session, and at one point has to hang on to her chair to prevent herself from walking up the aisle for a blessing, like some sort of demented bride. The girls look like they're in a state of rapture, crying and fainting. Hardly any boys go up, except a few soft-looking types who are already at a social disadvantage, being probably queer.

Mallory feels a sort of longing at these meetings that she can't understand. It's not like the longing for Cal or the longing to see her poetry in a literary journal or the longing to feel at least marginally pretty. This longing is different, a dangerous vacuum within.

She tries to write about all this, the only way she has ever been able to make sense of anything, not so much the Rev as the feel-ings he is stirring up in her, the yearning with no name. Showing what she has written to someone else turns out to be a big mistake.

GOD

Mallory does not know what she thinks about God.

Whether there really is one.

What he's like. Or she?

Could God be like her—a little of each?

Attempts to connect Mallory with a sense of God have failed, mainly because Mallory is too intelligent.

Sunday school made very little sense.

"Be careful, little hands, what you do
Be careful, little hands, what you do
For the Father up above
Is looking down in love
So be careful, little hands, what you do."

Mallory knows what this means. Don't touch the sensitive parts of your body, because it is a sin. It is a sin because of all the pleasure.

God does not want us to feel pleasure.

God wants shame.

God wants fear.

God wants absolute iron control.

But there is another one. Another sense. Another God? A God of William Blake and Gerard Manley Hopkins, of radical innocence and incandescent wonder. A God of the twinkling, starry hosts. A God of absolute awe. A God, even, of the rapture of orgasm.

Mallory is not unaware.

The Rev is full of that other kind of God. A dangerous God. Subversive, like Jesus flinging over the money-changer's tables in the temple, screaming and stamping with rage, driving out the merchants and their sacrificial animals with a nine-tailed whip.

Jesus, stamping and screaming. The Rev, pacing and raving and holding young girls in his powerful arms. So full of God he is about to split open, overflow the container, burst.

It jolts Mallory. She wonders if the two Gods could ever be one. They speak of the One, don't they? As if there is no division?

God observes Mallory in her world, her small but expanding, difficult, lonely world, and doesn't quite know what to think.

God knows Mallory was not a mistake, though she has yet to realize this herself. God also knows other things, such as the fact that the finest potential can sadly wink out. All too often, genius dies in the bud, snuffed out by a craven, undistinguished, greyly uniform world.

There is a way through.

But tenuous. Unsure. Involving choices.

It is never certain.

Yet there is a way, the merest bright thread of a way, which, if Mallory can only find the end of it, will take her through. Through to the other side of herself, to a form of completion.

God shows her the end.

MR. LIVINGSTON

"Mallory. I'm a little concerned about the things you've been writing lately."

Mallory sits in Mr. Livingston's empty classroom, hands demurely folded in her lap. She is wearing the brown ruffled blouse, which now frankly strains across the front.

Breasts are happening. Even a little bit of hip.

Mallory has not heard the expression *manwoman* for some time now. After what happened to Laura Cunningham, the other kids are not so quick to tease.

And Mallory's hair is longer. It even curls a bit around her collar, but she still will not wear makeup. A faint fur of moustache on her upper lip makes her look a little exotic.

Some men seem to like this, a hint of danger, of otherness. Of two sexual realities colliding in the same body. Impossibly, the bipolar extremes of male and female clothing themselves in the flesh of one person.

Mr. Livingston stares at her most recent essay.

Mighty strange stuff, for a young girl. In a way, she's writing almost at PhD level, freakishly advanced and sophisticated. The first time he really noticed this was when he read her essay on paradox in the poems of Dylan Thomas. It took him by surprise, as it was full of the kind of verbal acuity and insight he rarely found in a student: "In 'Fern Hill', the mature Dylan Thomas looks backward from the vantage-point of age thirty-two on the easy and dangerous ignorance of his youth," Mallory wrote. "The pastoral beauty of the poem disguises a lurking sense of predatory menace and the impending, irrevocable loss of Edenic innocence."

This is the kind of writing he has come to expect from Mallory. Vocabulary, usage, sentence structure, all are lively and impeccable, better than the majority of dry academic reading he has done. But at the same time, there is an uneven quality to the writing, an inconsistency, as if something crucial is strangely lacking. At a life-experience level, she is near zero, girlish and idealistic. Still caught up in fairy tales and enchantment, how she wishes things to be.

This latest essay is called "Radical Innocence: Concepts of the Divine as Expressed through the Poetic Imagination," and Mr. Livingston knows that this is a quotation from Yeats: "The soul recovers radical innocence/And learns at last that it is self-delighting ... "

How many fourteen-year-old girls are quoting William Butler Yeats in their essays?

But this piece is, strangely, all about God. Mr. Livingston never took Mallory for a religious girl, no, not at all.

Mr. Livingston himself is a secular humanist. Not quite an atheist, but certainly no believer. His intellectual experiences in college taught him that the existence of a Supreme Being is mostly a projection, the manifestation of a fervent human desire for a God above all. We created Him, not the other way around.

"But would it be so surprising," Mallory's essay states, "if there were indeed a Being watching over all our human affairs, a God not just of supremacy but of nature and the sensual world, a God of Blake, a God of Hopkins and of radical innocence? And could this God who presides over all be the same God that Dylan Thomas describes as 'the force that through the green fuse drives the flower'?"

Sheer naïveté. Fairy tales. Yet, in its own way, daring. There was more freshness, more originality of thought here than Mr. Livingston has seen in his classroom for the past fifteen years.

And it excites him.

It excites him in a way he can't quite express, or even fully comprehend.

He nearly believes what he tells himself, that Mallory is his protégé, and he her mentor. That he is performing a valuable role in her young life. Taking her under his wing.

He notices for the first time that Mallory is sitting up a little straighter, that her shape seems to be changing.

"What do you mean, concerned?" She fixes him with her bright uncanny eye, old eyes in a young face, unsettling. Her intense, slightly feverish gaze reminds Mr. Livingston of what he imagines the Ancient Mariner might look like.

"You're delving into areas that have frustrated some of the greatest minds of the literary world. God and the devil! Radical innocence! The courage of naïveté! Mallory, are you sure you feel qualified to comment on these things?"

"Don't I have as much right as anyone else?"

She has him there.

"But life experience has to match intellect. You're a precocious young girl, Mallory Mardling. Everybody knows how gifted you are."

"They do?" Mallory thinks of the used sanitary napkin some-one shoved in her locker when she wasn't looking. Though it has been muffled by fear, the campaign of terror has not ended. Every day Mallory must hold up a mighty shield to fend off the power-ful forces of social hate.

"If they don't, they soon will."

This gives Mallory a wild stab of hope. Ah, the demon hope! She has tried to suppress it in herself for as long as she can remember. Yet it has never quite worked. She can never com-pletely extinguish her spirit the way she'd like to. The thought of some kind of recognition ignites in her a wild craving that is worse than the pining for sex. If anything can be. Once lit, this flame will never die. This she knows, even with a mere fourteen years behind her.

"So I'll become this famous writer and people will fall on their knees and worship at my feet?"

Mr. Livingston smiles. Mallory sees he has an erection. It half excites and half disgusts her. She loves power and can't help but see her effect on him as power, of a physically transforming sort. Magic, really, to change a man's body part like that, to bring the blood.

"Not quite. Though I'm not so sure I'd rule out the famous writer part. It's important you find your forte, Mallory. Whether it's poetry—and I doubt that, your stuff is too strange—or academic writing, or perhaps some yet-unexplored form like playwriting or the novel."

"Aren't I a little young to be writing a novel?" The thought gives her a stab of wild exhilaration, however. *Christ! A novel?*

"You could begin with the short story, of course. In fact, I'd recommend it, as it's a somewhat less ambitious form. But in its way, no less challenging, due to the economy of expression needed to tell a complete story in a dozen pages."

Mallory has written short stories. Torn them up or burned them. They're all too sappy, all about Love, about meeting Someone. About two eyebeams twisting together on a single thread. Typical teenage bullshit, and she knows it.

"The thing is, Mallory, I see an imagination here that's in danger of running wild. You need to channel it into a form that has a little more creative scope than the essay. A short story can even have elements of the supernatural, such as you've presented in this piece you've given me. But believe me, it would all be a little more—what's the word?—palatable as a work of fiction."

God as a work of fiction.

"I'll try it," Mallory meekly tells him. Smiles demurely. God, she is learning. Learning how to make her own best ideas seem like someone else's. Learning to smile sweetly to get what she wants.

Maybe the therapy is working.

CAL

Mallory dreams of Cal and gets off spontaneously, her body shooting sparks like a rocket.

With him, she is extremely shy. Tentative. She lowers and raises her eyelids, though she does not know why she does this, some primitive pre-mating behaviour hard-wired into the core of her brain.

Cal is interesting. He smells gamey, which Mallory likes and is afraid of. He has, at least, read *The Catcher in the Rye.* There's some Holden in him, and Mallory wants to be Phoebe, even while knowing that that would be incest.

Cal plays with her.

She's standing around in Gail's rec room, stoned, but not much more stoned than usual, when Cal corners her.

He doesn't exactly corner her. He just stands there with his arm up on the door frame, sort of leaning into her, sexily.

"What's happenin', Mal?"

"Nothing."

"Hey, Mallory. I like your poetry."

"Thanks."

A beat.

"Hey, Cal?"

"Yeah."

"Do you ever ... you know. Do you ever write stuff?"

"Well." He looks a little embarrassed. Mallory notices the reddish stubble on his cheek and thinks it is painfully sexy. His hair is longish, a mane, and ginger-gold. His eyes, cat's-eye-marble blue.

"You do, don't you?"

"Everybody writes stuff."

Mallory feels a flare of irritation. Why does everyone treat writing like some dirty little secret?

"You write poetry." It's a statement, not a question.

"Shit, how'd you know that?"

"And I'll bet you keep a diary."

"Journal."

"Whatever. Can I . . . "

"I don't show my stuff to anyone."

"Why not?"

Cal stares into her stoned eyes. He takes one cool index finger and runs it down the side of her cheek, then over her neck. Her nipples harden like ice, like cherry stones, like the cold marble eyes of Michelangelo's David.

"It's not as good as your stuff, for one thing. I mean, you get A-pluses and all . . . "

"Not always."

"Mr. Livingston practically worships the ground you walk on, Mallory."

A tinge of sourness in the sweet.

"What are you saying?"

"He kind of plays favourites."

"Maybe he thinks I have some talent," Mallory snaps. By now she is getting bored and irritated with the conversation, and feels the familiar craving for a cigarette.

"Hey, listen. I know your shit is good. I've seen it. I just think Livingston's in love with you."

"Me? Christ, I'm a freak."

"Not really. I think you're getting kind of cute."

"*Cute?*" Mallory tries hard to act insulted.

"Y'know. Filling out and all. And you have a nice smile."

Mallory is incredulous.

"*When* you smile."

She wonders if all this is just charity. Or testing out his power over her. Or—is he actually interested? Curious? How much has Gail told the rest of the Club about what happened on the night of her initiation?

"But you're so smart, you scare guys away."

In some part of herself, Mallory already knows this.

"So am I supposed to act stupid?"

"I don't think you could."

"What, then? Plaster a bunch of makeup on?"

"I don't like a lot of makeup on girls. Makes 'em look like whores."

"You like Kathy. She wears makeup."

Cal looks a little startled.

"You're jealous."

"Of what?"

"Me 'n Kathy. We're just friends, y'know. We made it a couple of times, but it didn't mean anything."

"Then why did you do it?"

"I was *hor-ny*." He draws out the word, deep and husky.

"My God."

"Y'mean to say, you never get horny?"

"Shut *up*. This is so immature."

"I *know* you get horny, Mallory."

"What's Gail been saying?"

"Nothing." He moves in a hair closer. She can smell his breath now. Fear and desire clash, mingle. She feels dizzy, almost sick.

"You don't like girls, do you?" he murmurs in an embarrassingly intimate tone.

"Not really."

"Have you ever . . . "

"What business is it of yours? Creep!" But Mallory is enthralled and wants him to keep on asking her questions. Wants him to kiss her all over her body. Everywhere. The soles of her feet. Her armpits. The nape of her neck.

"So you're still cherry."

"I think I rode too many horses for that."

Cal finds this wildly funny and bursts into stoned laughter.

"Bareback, eh, Mallory?"

"Drop dead."

"You like me."

He has her there.

As if to prove it, he lunges forward and plants a quick but firm kiss on her mouth.

The other kids are starting to notice. Bob Dylan is wailing on the stereo in the background, "Positively Fourth Street," the lyrics deadly as viper toxin. Kathy's not there tonight, thank God. Probably seeing a probation officer or something.

The two of them are on their own private island.

He dips to kiss again.

This time, lips a little open.

She responds.

He nuzzles. Mallory shivers.

She feels his face-prickles on her hot skin and flushes deeply. Her body in flames.

He tries again. This time he goes in. Mallory has never felt a boy's tongue in her mouth before and at first she resists, unable to accomodate the powerful sensation. The strangeness. Repulsion at this big wet worm wriggling its insistent way inside her. Yet things are happening to her, physiological changes, things she is powerless to control. She is swelling and fizzing and wetting slickly, as if possessed by the demon Sex.

She wants *more*.

Then he pulls back. Starts walking away.

"See you, Mallory."

God!

And they say girls tease. Yet she knows in her soul that she has somehow made all this happen herself.

It sparks and steams like a pressure in her head, in her breast.

Power.

THE DEMON

Mallory can't believe this.

Anika Voortman is hanging around with Simon.

Snake-eyes Simon, the scariest guy she's ever seen.

Simon with the motorcycle. Simon with the handcuffs. When Anika shows up at the Club with a small black cobra tattooed on her pale upper arm, everyone is impressed.

But here's the strange thing, the murky thing. Anika's taking Simon to church with her, to hear the Rev's talks. No one can quite believe that Simon would ever show up in a church, even in the basement. But he sits through it all and says things like "Far out." He agrees that Jesus was cool. Preaching peace, love, acceptance and understanding.

But Simon has no idea of the power that is being released here.

Things happen at these meetings, and that's why the kids keep coming back. Mallory is enthralled. Watching people is her sport, but watching them come apart is beyond fascinating.

The Rev strides up and down. He sweats. He rants. Like Lord Buckley the beat poet, he sometimes calls Jesus *the Nazz*.

"To be in the hands of the Nazz, to be touched by the Nazz, to feel the sweet kiss of the Nazz on your weary brow, I tell you, my children, and I tell you this truly, verily, verily I say unto you, it's heaven indeed. He will heal you, my children. He'll take away all that awful despair that you feel when your parents are fighting all night and you can hear the shouting in the next room. He'll heal all your loneliness and pain when you feel like nobody in the world understands you or cares about you or knows what you're all about. He'll *walk* with you and he'll *talk* with you and he'll show you the way to a Paradise right here on this earth."

The air vibrates. Mallory feels a low-grade quiver like a storm warning, a sense that something is about to blow.

"Who will be the first?" The Rev is really worked up now, whipping his jacket off and tearing open the neck of his shirt. "Who will be the first to receive the Kingdom of Heaven? Who will lay themselves bare? Who will make the sacrifice? Who will throw down their earthly garments and run to Him?"

"*Jeeeeeeee-sus!*"

Jesus.

It's Anika. Screaming.

Simon tries to pull her back down into her chair, but it's too late, the genie is already out of the bottle and now there is no going back.

She stands rapt, her amber eyes a yellow fire. "Jesus," she wails, "heal me, Jesus."

"Come forward, Annie. Annie, Anika, that's it, that's my girl. Oh sweet Annie, come to me! Don't be ashamed to cry. Your Lord will heal you tonight." She staggers forward, tear-blind, and sinks to her knees in front of the Rev, whose face is flushed and crumpled up with compassion and something else that Mallory can't even name.

"Jesus," Anika weeps.

"Yes, Annie. You don't need to be afraid, because the Demon knows him by name."

The *what?*

Mallory starts, in terror and recognition. A thrill of shock whips around the room from body to body like chain lightning.

"He knows the Lord by name. Say his name."

"Jesus."

"*Say* his name."

"Jesus!"

"*Say my name!*"

"Oh JesuschristthelordfortheloveofGod, save me," Anika blurts, unable to keep the words inside her any more.

"Let this sweet girl go."

Annie's face contorts and an ungodly scream rips from the depth of her throat. The room freezes.

"Let God's servant Annie go. In the name of all that's holy, I command you ..."

What is he *doing?*

Mallory flashes back to Victor in the bedroom. The way he circled her chair.

Annie looks like death, her skin grey, her eyes fixed. Her mouth opens and closes, but no sound comes out.

"Come out of her."

An appalling silence.

"Come *out!*"

"No," Annie wails.

"Don't fight, my girl. Let the power of the Holy Spirit root this evil being out of your heart. I command you, in the name of the Father, in the name of the Son, in the name of the Holy Ghost: OUT!"

Her head jerks back, her jaws unhinge, and something comes flying out of her mouth.

(Mallory wonders: *Am I going crazy? Do the others see this?*)

Something comes flying out of her mouth like a ball of black fire blown out of a cannon, hurtles across the room and explodes with an ear-splitting, sulphurous *crack*, leaving an ashy plume that stinks like a spent firecracker.

And everyone is turning around to look.

Annie buckles. She goes boneless. The Rev bends down to touch her blonde head, to pray over her.

But the words don't make any sense.

A thin, just-visible reek is rising in the far corner of the room. Which is now dead-frozen. No one knows how to move.

"Maranatha, natha ma-nara ben jimzen, manara jimzen jem bon. Benatha, mala natha ..."

Annie can't get up.

Simon jumps to his feet. "Hey."

The Rev holds up his hand.

"*Talitha cum.* Get up, little girl."

She sits up, jerkily and fast, like a doll on a string.

A gasp goes round the room. Then a large, collective sigh.

Annie's face breaks open in a wide, childish smile. An almost thermal warmth drenches the room. Solar. Benevolent. Mighty.

The Rev helps Annie to her feet.

Simon starts the applause. One set of hands clapping. Then two. Then another, and another. And then it's bedlam.

Clapping, and cheering, and girls crying, and boys roaring and bellowing and stomping their feet, and Annie moving down into the crowd to receive hugs and touches.

Annie. Annie. Annie.

She's a superstar.

Mallory sits entranced. She wonders if Victor should take lessons from this guy.

And if this guy could fix whatever's wrong with *her*. Whatever that is.

She still smells the sulphur. It happened. They all saw it.

The Rev pushes through the milling crowd and lays his hand on her head for just one blazing second. Mallory feels as if she has been hit with a board.

A lurching smack of *power*.

GRAMMA, OUT

Gramma should have died years ago.

She keeps almost dying, then being brought back to life again with needles of adrenalin shot straight into her heart.

Gramma has been in a home for years. Mum doesn't make her go see her too often. This is good, for the smell of Dettol and stale pee and old flesh, the prehistoric howls of the stroke patients, freak Mallory right out.

Gramma doesn't know who Mallory is.

"Who's this boy?" Her sour and hollow voice a parody of what it once was.

"Mother. That's *Mallory*. Your granddaughter."

"Where's Victor?"

"Victor isn't feeling well, Mother." Victor is hanging upside down like a bat from a beam in the basement, singing to himself about smokes and tokes and watching *Captain Kangaroo*. He won't take his medication. They've had to take the Bunsen burner away from him so he won't burn the place down.

Victor did something weird. Something scary. He showed himself to Mallory. Mallory did not want to see. His thing looked huge. Mallory could not believe a male member could grow to that size. She said "Oh, for Christ's *sake*, Victor, zip yourself up," and walked away, more scared than she could say.

Gramma smells like the bottom of an old bureau drawer. Mallory tries to love her the way she used to, but finds it a struggle. She seems so small. Smaller than the last time she came to visit. You can see her pulsating scalp through the sparse strands of yellow-white hair. She looks more like a man, or less like a woman. Her body is shrivelling, her mind connected by a single thread, yet her essence still hangs around her, unable to move on.

Oldness is strange. The body dries out, curves, dies by inches. Mum talks at Gramma, brightly. It is horribly artificial and false. But everyone in the nursing home is artificial and false with the residents, as if that is what they want.

Almost everything has fallen away, except for a pulse. Toilet habits. The ability to be social. Even simple recognition of loved ones. All this Mallory sees. Sees and sees. So much of what she sees appalls her. Yet everyone expects her to be happy. The fact that she is not happy is a major problem.

This going to the psychiatrist every Wednesday after school is an attempt to make her be happy.

If she is happy, then she will be quiet. No more crying. And maybe she will look less weird in the deal.

Gramma gapes at Mallory, her mouth a slack, black cave. "Get that boy away."

"Mother. It's *Mallory*. You remember Mallory. Mallory, talk to her."

Mallory leans over the bedrail. "Gramma! Gramma, it's me. *Mallory*."

"Mallory."

It is the last thing Gramma says. For just then, something happens.

Her eyes jerk backward in her skull, her breath pulls jaggedly inward in a long deep ratcheting snore, and an instant later, she dies.

Mallory sees her die.

"Mother. Oh Mother. Nurse! Nurse! She's taking a spell."

Two nurses come running. They take her pulse. One of them listens to her chest with a stethoscope. The older nurse looks at the younger one and shakes her head a little, her lips pressed together.

"But isn't there anything you can *do?*" Mum is beside herself. Mallory notices a large glowing ball of energy pulling up out of the middle of Gramma's chest and drifting up towards the ceiling.

"We're sorry, Mrs. Mardling. Last time we brought her back we broke seven of her ribs. She kept saying *let me go, let me go*. Dr. Danforth told us not to do that again."

Mum is totally stunned. So the doctor ordered them to let her die. Mum does not argue with doctors. But she is still stunned.

"She's tired, Mrs. Mardling. She's nearly a hundred years old. It's time for her to go."

"But she can't just . . ."

The nurses are pulling a sheet up over Gramma's head, just like in the movies. Mallory is fascinated. Her mother is whimpering with panic and grief.

Dead. What does it mean to be dead? Mallory looks up at the glowing ball hovering just below the ceiling. That's Gramma, that's what she was for ninety-seven years or however long, just that, pure energy in a flesh packet. The energy made the flesh packet "go." Now the energy is "out." It will hang around for a while, and a few people, only a few, will feel their neck hairs standing erect and wonder why they felt Muriel Anderson's presence in the room when everyone knew she was dead.

Mallory sometimes wants to be dead: free, "out." She still cuts herself a little, but shallow, feeble cuts. She hasn't burned herself in a while. Perhaps the social contact is helping. That's what Dr. Rubens says. The best way to cancel yourself is pills, but then again, you might pull through. A razor blade is too awful, too much gore. Mallory should know. And if there is a God, might this God judge you for throwing away your one and only, irreplaceable life?

Mallory can sometimes imagine a different sort of life for herself as a published author. She would do readings at literary festivals, she'd make money and everyone would admire her. She would no longer inspire that blank look, that look of puzzlement. She would no longer have to simplify her vocabulary, her personality, to make it more acceptable to others.

She would live with her black lover Vernon in a loft in Montreal, or maybe even Paris, with a pet iguana named Rico. Children? They'd be caramel-coloured. No, scratch the children. A pet ocelot, which she'd walk on a leash.

Though she knows they are incredibly stupid, these daydreams hold back the impulse to take all her pills, to be dead like

Gramma. She tries to write a poem about her, but the words will not come, they seem to resist her. So she writes the poem she can write, a sort of replica of what she longs to say.

She dreads being old like Gramma, a dessicated relic, all her moisture sucked away. Tenderness vies with revulsion as she wrestles with the words.

> to be old like you are old:
> all juice sucked dry, your face
> like the skin of dried apricots
> sweetish furred flesh
> in a state of soft decay

At the funeral, Mallory doesn't cry, though perhaps she is expected to. She feels almost good. Gramma is "out." *Free.* No more body to feed and water and walk, no more lusts or itches to satisfy. Nothing to clothe or bathe. Think of the time saved, the energy. She wonders why people hang on to life with such ferocity, when *dead* has so many obvious advantages.

As in Mallory's dreams where she is completely disembodied, a ball of pure energy, Gramma's essence drifts around for a while. Then it moves on. No one knows what or where this "on" is. But it is not here. And it is not now. It is not a place and not a time, but another sort of reality.

> you smell stale as a used apron
> or the bottom of a bureau drawer
>
> (and under the paper lining
> a valentine pressed flat, its crumbling lace
> bleached pale with time
> its faint gold script
> shining across the century:
> "Be joy forever near thee")

Mr. Livingston tells me I should write fiction. I will not tell him this, not yet anyway, but I have started a novel. Well, maybe a novella. Who knows. It's called THE SECRET OF SILVERNOR, OR MAID MADELEINE'S HONOUR, and it's all about this magical city, this Kingdom of Silvernor suffering under the rule of a dark King, a pretender to the throne who is oppressing everyone, especially the children. I know people are going to think it's a kid's story, but it isn't, any more than THE LORD OF THE RINGS is for children, it's way beyond that level, but who's going to understand what I'm trying to do here? I have this character in it, a really important character named Maid Madeleine the Fair and Powerful, not fair like a maiden in a tower but fair like a judge, and she's kind of a seer, she can see into the future, a wizard actually, not a witch, that's too much of a cliché, but I can just hear them saying I can't do that, a girl can't be a wizard, it's not allowed, you need a knight in shining armour and all that crap, and not this sad-faced young prophet with the haunting eyes. But Maid Madeleine just came into my head out of nowhere and now I feel like I know her personally, so I can't let her go, or she won't let *me* go, I don't know which.

I know it's all a bunch of shit. I can tell that every time I work on it, but still, every time I work on it I disappear. I just sort of phase out. It's not like I forget everything, it's not like time dissolves, that's a cliché too. It's more like I'm "not," as if there are no barriers, no veil of flesh, and I am pure energy. Yeah, I know, that sounds like shit too.

Then I go see Dr. Rubens for "therapy." This consists of sitting in the room and figuring out what she wants me to say, what she'd like to hear, so I can pass for normal and get the hell away from her. She asked to see my arms the other day, and I told her I couldn't, I had a rash, but she made me pull my sleeves up anyway, and she saw scars. Some old razor marks and some blisters and burns, but mostly well healed-over, so it's hard to tell what they originally were.

"You haf been hurting yourself," she stated. She didn't ask. I thought this was sort of disrespectful.

"What makes you think I've been hurting myself?" This was a deliberate parody of her particular style of interrogation, but it sailed right over her permy old head.

"Mallory. Zese are sca-ars." That's how she pronounced it. *Sca-ars.* "How else vould you get zem?"

"The dog bit me."

"Mallory, you don't haf a dog."

"The cat, then."

For some reason she finds this amusing. She suppresses a smirk, making her look sort of like a vindictive elf.

"Vee need to explore vhy you feel the need to ha-arm yourself."

"Maybe I fucking hate myself."

"Mallory!"

"Well, it's true. Aren't we supposed to try to get at the truth?"

"Such lenguage." She looks scared. I don't blame her. Sometimes I scare myself.

"Vhy vould a talented young gerrl like you feel such hatred for herself?" She takes off her glasses and starts to clean them, a theatrical gesture meant to distract attention away from her face. It isn't working.

"You are geefted, Mallory. In many vays, you are an exceptional young vhoman."

"But I'm a freak." Sometimes the truth just sort of comes out. I hate it.

"You haf friends. They accept you."

"But they're freaks, too." I start to cry and it totally shames me. I feel so weak. Dr. Rubens hands me the box of Kleenex.

"Vell, at last maybe vee start to get somevheres," she mutters to herself. She has broken down my defenses at last.

So she begins to talk, while I snuffle and sniff.

She begins to talk about vhat it is to be a Vhoman.

It's interesting in a way, because it sort of reminds me of Mum. A vhoman's purpose is to be a support to her mate, to build up his confidence, to raise and nurture his children, to look attractive, to speak low and be agreeable.

Intellectual pursuits are not ruled out, of course. A vhoman must keep herself interesting for her husband, so he won't be tempted to stray. Like Scheherezade, she can keep him enthralled with a thousand and one tales of

Nietszche and Heidegger and Einstein's Theory of Relativity. But zees pursuits must never subsume her primary task, which is to look after her mate and her family, to prepare the next generation of sons for future greatness.

"Dr. Rubens. May I ask you something?"

"Of course, Mallory."

"Are you married?"

She looks flustered.

"Divorced."

"Any children?"

"No." Her face is turning as many colours as an octopus in distress. I half expect her to start squirting ink.

"Why did you decide to become a psychiatrist?"

"Mallory. Vee are getting distracted here."

"I'm just curious."

"The path of my life ..." She can't seem to finish the thought. "The plans vee make for our lives do not always materialize in quite the vay vee expected."

"So you should always have something to fall back on?"

"Why—yes."

"Such as—your brain."

"Intelligence in a vhoman is to be highly prized."

"But you're telling me to get married, have babies and shut up."

"Mallory. Be honest with me. Don't you ever dream of being married?"

I have never once pictured myself in a long white gown. When I was supposed to be playing bride, I was busy collecting tadpoles in jars and watching them metamorphose into frogs. Married? Never. Shacked up, I can see. I remember Vernon, my black lover from the Parisian fantasy.

"No."

"The security, the sense of fulfillment ..."

"How long were you married?"

"I vas married ..." She counts in her head. "Six years."

"Why did you get divorced?"

"Mallory."

"Was it a big wedding?"

I have thrown her completely off balance. She looks close to tears. I feel a mean sense of triumph.

But I also feel like shit.

Really, I'm not that bad. And just because everybody's mean to me, does that mean I have the right to be crappy back at them? Isn't this lady trying to help me? All right, she gets paid for it, it's her job to try to help me, but something must have drawn her into psychiatry in the first place, and the path might have been easier if she'd gone into nursing or teaching.

"Sorry, Dr. Rubens. That wasn't fair."

She looks shredded, almost undone. "Mallory, zere must be respect."

"I do respect you. I think it's cool that you're a shrink. You sort of broke the mould. But I don't know why you have to push marriage so hard. I'm pretty young to be thinking about all that stuff, aren't I? I mean, I'd like to have a boyfriend and all ..." Even though Cal kissed me all the way down into the soles of my feet, I have no illusions. I know he is not my boyfriend.

"Do you find boys attractive?" That again.

"You think I'm queer."

"Mallory, please do not jump to conclusions."

I know I'm not queer. I even had a chance to find out. "No, I like boys. I like them a lot. It's just that I don't want to think about getting married at fourteen years old."

She seems to find this reasonable. I can tell by her face. It feels for a minute like we might almost be connecting, and it gives me a weird sort of hope, like I sometimes get talking to Mr. Livingston. (Kenneth. Ken. *Kenny.*) I want somebody to hear me. And I feel like nobody does. Maybe that's why I write so much.

So I tell her about my novel and I see this look on her face, the weirdest mixture of real interest and reluctance. Like she should be telling me to take up knitting or try out for cheerleaders or something. Yet the Brontë sisters wrote, and Jane Austen, and and ... Surely she sees it as a suitable feminine pursuit, so long as I don't get out of hand and try to publish it or something?

"Zis is a good hobby," she says, affirming my thought.

"But I want to write. It's the only thing I do really well. And I feel good when I'm doing it."

"But Mallory, just as you are young to be thinking of marriage, you are young to be vorking out your vocation."

I'm not sure what to say to this.

"But I should practise. In case I end up being a writer."

92

"I zee nothing wrong with zis." She looks surreptitiously at her watch. Our time is nearly up.

And I haven't even told her about Gramma. I thought I would miss her. I thought I would grieve. But I feel okay about it, kind of a sense of peace. Relief, almost. I'm not glad she's dead or anything, I'm not that big a shit. But I am glad she isn't in that horrible old body any more, struggling to draw her next breath. I do think I hear her voice sometimes in a crowd, but I look around and it's somebody else.

And when I was out walking the other day by myself, I felt her. I couldn't make out any words or see her face or anything, I just felt her, and it was warm and reassuring, like: *Mallory, don't worry. Everything's going to be okay.* And I cried. Not because I was sad, but because that's how I used to feel as a little girl when she'd put her hand on my head to steady herself walking. She'd say *oh bless her heart.* And I'd feel okay in myself, for once. Like it was all right to be me.

I don't tell Dr. Rubens about any of this stuff. It's private. None of her business. Most of the stuff I tell her is intended to throw her off the scent.

But isn't it possible that some day, somewhere, somehow, somebody will finally hear me?

ANNIE HAD A BABY

And then something big. Something strange.

Mallory finds out in the bathroom, where so many things happen.

The bathroom is where you go to cry at lunch hour in school. Where you go to put on some of the new makeup you just bought at the Metropolitan. Yardley's Sigh Shadow in Not So Innocent Blue.

But it's also a place for secrets.

A bunch of them are sitting around in the Satellite Restaurant, eating French fries and talking about acid, which Mallory has never done.

Kathy has, about a hundred times, and tries to convince her: "Aw, c'mon. It'd be fun."

"I'm just afraid I'd fry my brain or something."

Cal leers at her and Mallory starts getting turned on. "C'mon, Mal. I'd like to see you tripping." Sometimes she fucking hates him, hates the effect he has on her, which is hard to control. She wonders if that is why some men seem to hate women so much. Or is it fear? All that spooky witchy power to make the blood surge and the mind cloud.

Cal keeps pressing her. "You wouldn't even have to pay for it. It'd be on me."

"Lay off, Cal." Gail looks annoyed. Maybe she's a little jealous.

"I'm going to the ladies' room," Annie announces to everyone. She looks at Mallory.

Mallory doesn't get it.

"I don't have to go."

"Mallory!" It's a signal, a code, a—something. Kathy would get it, but only because she's more like normal, or at least she looks more like normal. Mallory is not used to girlfriend behaviour, all this business of sharing confidences in the can.

"Oh. Okay." She looks around at everyone and they all have this look on their faces that she cannot decipher.

Cal says in a heavy seductive voice, "Have a good time, Mallory."

She sticks her tongue out at him and he wags his tongue back at her, and it is for all the world as if he is wagging his penis.

Annie and Mallory both pee. It strikes her as strange that you'd go off together to a pissing place, but Annie obviously has something to say to her.

Then they're washing their hands at the sink. Mallory sticks on some lipstick for something to do, and Annie preens the way pretty girls do in front of a mirror.

"I'm late."

"Late?" For a genius, Mallory can be a little thick.

"You know."

"My God."

"Like, two months have gone by and nothing. And look at my boobs, they're huge."

"What are you going to do?"

"Shit. I dunno."

"Who did it?"

"Mallory!"

"I mean . . . who's the father?"

"Uh, I think it's Simon."

"You *think*?"

Annie is turning every colour. She's hiding something.

Mallory narrows her eyes at her.

Then she knows.

"It's the Rev."

"Mallory! Shut the fuck up."

But she has scored a direct hit, and now Annie is crying.

"Christ, Annie, why'd you go to bed with an old man?"

"He took advantage of me."

"I'll bet."

"It was . . . I mean, he made it seem so special."

"Being knocked up isn't so special."

"I'm thinking maybe I can get a summer job somewhere, go away for a couple months . . ."

"But by the time you came back, you'd be out to here." Mallory gestures in front of her stomach.

"I don't know what the hell to do. I wanted to be a camp counsellor this summer."

"*You?*"

It stings her momentarily, then they both burst out laughing.

"Sorry."

"S'okay. You're probably right, a pregnant freak shouldn't be counselling kids."

"Are you going to tell youknowwho?"

"I'd get him in trouble."

"I'd say he already is. Christ, Annie, he shouldn't be having sex with kids."

"But he's different. You saw what he did for me. I've been carrying that thing around inside me all my life."

"What thing?"

"You know. The demon."

"Demon, shmeemon. That was just show biz."

"You saw it, Mal."

Annie has her there. Something did happen and they all saw it, even smelled it.

"Yeah, but what good is being exorcized if you're knocked up? What'll you do with the baby?"

"Don't worry, I won't sacrifice it." At this they laugh again, but Annie's laugh is blubbery and unbalanced.

"You could, you know, get an abortion. Nola had one. They lied and said she was having a nervous breakdown and that having a baby would endanger her mental health."

Annie looks reflective for a second.

"But it's a sin."

"And fucking the Rev wasn't?"

"He made it seem like it was okay. Like we were doing God's will, almost."

"Christ. That's scary. He has you hypnotized."

"He's like really intense. I think he's a genius."

"Can't keep it in his pants, more like."

"Mallory."

"Yeah?"

"Have you ever?"

Mallory is flustered. "Yeah, of course I have. Or how would I be in the Club?"

"Everybody knows you and Gail just talked."

"What else did she say?"

"Nothing." A beat. "Just that you were a little . . . unusual."

"*Fuck.*" Mallory feels like she is being turned inside out.

"Relax. We're all fuckups in this group. That's what we have in common."

"But you're so pretty." Now it's Mallory's turn to get blubbery.

"Pretty. Right. A lot of good it does me. My stepfather won't stay out of my bedroom."

"Your parents are divorced?"

"My dad died."

"Anika!"

"Yeah, no shit. Drove his car into a tree. They said it was an accident. Doesn't bother me. I'm over it." She jabs at her mouth with bright red lipstick.

"That must be . . ."

"Look, don't feel sorry for me. Could be worse. Could be my stepdaddy's kid, but you can't get pregnant from a blow job."

"Anika. That must be horrible."

"It is." She slams out of the washroom, the door thudding shut on her little room of confidences.

Mallory stands there for a while, staring into the mirror, wondering how things can get so fucked up. Easy, apparently. Let sex get out of control, as it always wants to, and there is hell to pay.

She never really liked Annie but sort of admired her, and always thought she was pretty and confident in a bossy big-sister way.

And Mallory thinks she has it bad at home.

INTERLUDE

There are only a few things that happen to people. Only a few. There are not that many plots. It all goes round and round, and everybody thinks they're being so original.

So Mallory thinks. You get pregnant. No, you "get yourself pregnant." Everyone says so. The guy has no role to play in it at all.

You're born, you flail around for a while, and then you die. There are little things along the way, flashes of insight, even awe. Sometimes pleasure is so intense that it makes a mockery of pain. But is that enough?

Girls really get fucked over. That much is evident. Is that why God made her half boy? Is this some sort of weird saving grace?

But she won't realize that until much later.

FANTASIES

Annie and the Rev, *take one:*

"Annie. You're a very special young woman. And God made you in a very special way."

"I never felt special before."

"Your skin is a miracle. Feel how soft. Go on, Annie, feel the skin on your neck. Now this."

He guides her hand over her upper chest.

"Now this."

He pulls down her tank top to reveal two firm, hard-nippled young breasts.

His mouth closes over one nipple. He groans. Annie gasps. Then Mallory can see his bald head bobbing up and down like a lifebuoy, and it's all over.

Take two:

"Annie. God made us both in a miraculous way, to fit together. Like this."

No. Screw that, it's stupid.

Take three:

"Annie. Annie. Annie."

"Dolph. I love you, Dolph."

The two of them writhe and heave. Too obvious?

Take four:

"Annie, you are fearfully and wonderfully made."

Annie opens her blouse to him.

"You look like a blonde madonna." He pushes back her long fair hair.

"This is my first time." She's blushing.

"Then I promise I'll be gentle."

She falls over backwards on the bed, and the Rev's big body covers her.

And *oh*

Oh yes.

Ohhhhhhh . . . *yes.*

THE POINT OF ALL THIS

Sometimes Mallory hates the way she is. All fucky. Everything is sex. But it isn't, not really. There is the life of the mind, and it's burgeoning. She is writing more than ever now. And all of it is good. That is, when it isn't turning to shit before her very eyes. Then it's a miracle in reverse, wine into water, and dirty water at that.

Mr. Livingston has made a grab more than once, or tried to. He has tried to set something up, get her alone in his house or even in his car. Mallory is evasive, eelish, quick to dart away. The game is becoming scary now, as if it might get out of hand.

It's near the end of the school year and he keeps running possible scenarios by her: come sailing with me on the weekend. Come on a picnic. Yeah, right, a picnic of two. Bottle of wine. Condoms. Roughing it in the bush. She remembers the old joke from grade five about the little girl peeing next to the little boy: "That's a handy thing to have at a picnic."

But what is she going to do over the summer? She's too young to get a job, unless she lies like Annie (who actually did get the camp counselling job. She told her mother she's just fat from Cherry Blossoms and Coke. The idiot believed her. Parents.).

Cal keeps teasing her, cornering her and making out just a little, feeling her up—God, is he a good kisser. Where did he learn that technique? He plays the saxophone, and there's just something sexual about being a musician, a performer, up there in the spotlight, even if it is just a dumb smelly old high school gymnasium, something about the way he wraps his lips around that gooseneck, and even though his playing is mostly obscene honks, Mallory gets turned on watching him bob up and down in some sort of bizarre public mating dance.

But she can't delude herself that they're together. The idea makes her laugh.

He is far below her intellectually, anyway. Not worth her time. Sometimes she even hangs out with Simon the Snake, who is surprisingly smart for a reptile.

"Hey, Simon."

"Hey, Mallory. What's happenin'?"

"Did you ever wonder what the point of all this is?"

"Point of what?"

"Of—whatever. Of anything."

"You mean all this life shit?"

"Yeah, I guess."

"Uh, well I guess we're s'posed to hang out and have a good time and—"

"Aren't we supposed to be making a contribution to the world or something? I mean—"

"Look, Mallie." (She loves it when he calls her Mallie. He's the only one who does. Makes her feel like she exists or something.) "I used to think I was gonna make some sort of great contribution with my art." Simon makes sculptures and stuff out of old bicycle parts, things like that. You can play some of them like musical instruments. Mallory thinks they're cool.

"So why don't you?"

"I gave up on it because I never got any, you know, recognition." Simon is seventeen. "It's all shit, anyway, the art world. It'll be different for you, though."

"Why do you say that?"

"Your stuff is really good. We all think so."

"I think it's shit."

"All artists think that. Probably proves that you're good."

"It does?"

"You know you're gonna keep doin' it, no matter what happens."

"Yeah, you're probably right about that."

"So it's, like, your destiny."

"What if it doesn't sell?"

"Who gives a shit?"

"I do. I want to be successful."

"You're some piece of work, Mallory. But I like you."

"You're scary as hell, Simon. But you're okay."

"That's the nicest thing you've ever said to me."

"Can the sarcasm."

"No, I mean it. You're pretty cool. Way cooler than you think you are."

This makes her a little bit mad, a little bit sad, and a little bit glad.

BUSTED

At the next session with the Rev, Mallory is ready.

She's going to get the bastard. Get him for what he did to Annie. And to who knows how many other young girls who sit breathless and exalted each week as he works his particular, sweaty magic on the crowd.

Mallory has to push past a group of stoners hanging around the church basement door.

One of them reeks of booze, even at a distance. "Hey, where's the Rev?" he slurs.

His buddy can barely stand up. "Prob'ly fuckin' somebody."

"Shut *up*, you guys." Mallory's eyes flare at them.

"What're you, jealous?"

"You guys should shape up. You look disgusting."

"Hey, the Rev says we should enjoy our young bodies. Have a snort, kid." This freaky-looking guy with whitish frizz for hair holds out a slimy mickey of Southern Comfort. She shoves past him, shooting him a look of contempt.

The crowd is almost hysterical tonight. It's a weird vibe. The air is thick with it. Too rambunctious. Mallory wonders if the Rev feels a need to up the ante. An exorcism one week, water into wine the next?

Is he going to heal the sick, raise the dead, drive the little girls out of their heads?

But he seems a little subdued this time when he walks out.

The usual flash and blast is dimmed down. The mob, which up to now has been groaning like an animal, hushes down and holds its breath.

"You beautiful young people," the Rev says, his eyes shining with what might be tears. "Tonight I want to talk to you about sin."

"Shit!" somebody says.

Mallory thinks: What's this *sin* stuff? She wonders if the party's over. Kathy is rolling her eyes. Everybody looks confused.

"Sin, my children, is anything that divides you from the grace of God. Sin is anything that causes you shame or remorse. Sin is that which keeps you from living the passionate kind of life that God wants you to live."

Mallory looks around the room and notices stunned expressions: *what the fuck?*

"You might have heard in Sunday school that it's a sin to love another human being in the way God designed us to love. You may have heard that it's a sin to touch your own body, the parts that our Creator filled with sensation and delight. I say to you, my beautiful friends, that feeling ashamed of these natural impulses is the only sin! We were made to love each other and made to love our own beautiful, miraculous bodies. Made to glory in the miracle of the flesh, in the mystery of male and female. When we feel guilty about these things, God shakes his head in frustration. God pleads with us for understanding. God wants us to *love!*"

"What's he getting at?" Kathy whispers to Mallory.

Mallory knows.

And on and on he goes. When it's all about sex, the group gets quiet, enthralled. Then it comes time to go up to the front to receive the blessing, and for the first time Mallory actually gets up from her seat. But for a reason, a different reason from salvation.

The other girls are crying. Probably a lot of them have put out for their boyfriends, or at least touched themselves under the covers, learning slowly by feel exactly what it takes to get themselves off. A couple of guys go up, as usual, one with such bad skin that it makes Mallory wonder if there's truth in the old wives' tale about self-abuse.

Mallory makes sure she stands at the very front of the room, so close to the Rev that she can feel his body heat and smell his sweat, which carries a strong whiff of alcohol.

He raises his hands over the crowd of weeping, kneeling teenagers. Mallory stands straight as a sapling and looks him in the eye.

"You're busted," she murmurs.

For a split second the Rev has a puzzled, what-are-you-saying look on his face, along with a hint of suppressed panic.

"Busted." Just so he knows for sure that it wasn't a mistake.

"See me after," he mouths, then focusses his high beams on his disciples. "Gracious God, bless these young people today as they walk in your love . . ."

Mallory waits around after the service, and waits very patiently as all the young women come up to the Rev one by one, weepily, wanting to talk to him about their own particular sins. When the crowd has thinned out, he gestures to Mallory and leads her into a side room, his dressing room, she guesses, as it has black robes and things hanging on coat hangers. She sees a half-empty bottle of Gilbey's gin and realizes that's probably what she can smell.

"Now."

Mallory stares at him.

"What seems to be the problem, Mallory?"

A thick pause.

"I know about Annie."

The Rev is not that good a liar, for before he can suppress it, a stricken look flashes across his face.

"I don't know what you're talking about."

"Yes, you do. She talked to me the other day. I know all about it."

"Mallory. Annie comes from a broken home. Her stepfather's not a kind man. He takes advantage of her in all kinds of unpleasant ways."

"And you don't?"

"Mallory, this is a very serious accusation you are making."

"You bet it is."

"But you have no basis for it."

"I have Annie's word."

"Annie's a very troubled young woman."

"I know she is. And I know why."

"Mallory, whatever concerns you have about Annie, I think you'd better keep them to yourself. You know what I've been saying about talking to the grown-ups. It just isn't a good idea, because they wouldn't understand. Annie has a very vivid imagination about many things. I happen to know that she looks up to me as a protector."

"Then you're doing a hell of a job." Mallory doesn't know where this courage is coming from.

The Rev looks profoundly uncomfortable. For once he seems to be at a loss for words.

"She's pregnant, you know."

Then she realizes he didn't. *Oh shit.*

"Mallory . . ." His smell is slowly turning rank. "Annie has talked to me about her promiscuity."

"I thought sex was a miracle of God."

"Sarcasm doesn't become you, Mallory." But he is afraid of her. She can tell.

"You're basically telling us all to go out there and screw. But you don't talk about birth control or VD or anything like that."

"I'm talking about love, Mallory."

"Shame on you." She gives him a hard look. "Shame."

He doesn't know what to say.

Then she turns and walks. And sees Annie on her way out of the church, her face swollen from crying.

Shit. It's all shit. The grown-ups, Annie and the Rev, her fucking parents, Victor masturbating his brains out every day, all of it, all *all all* of it. She walks the seven blocks home and slams into her room and puts a record on the turntable. Janis Joplin screeching wild, pumped full of drugs and Southern Comfort and swollen with sexual heat like an animal in season. She banshees her way through "Ball and Chain" with raw flames spurting out of her voice, ripping into the heartblasted lyrics with a great hulking chainsaw of pain.

If I could sing like that. I might be okay. *If I could sing like that.* I might not be lonely. *If I could sing like that.* Or do anything like

that. That well. That purely. With that kind of ravishing intensity. The woman is a gift. But doomed. Mallory feels doomed.
Blackness creeps in on her. There is a cold spot in the middle of
her chest and it's spreading. Even cutting her arms with the
paper-doll scissors or burning herself with a cigarette is not going
to make her feel any better. She wants to take all her pills but only
has seven left in the bottle, not enough to do the job. She wants
to pull all the hair out of her *fucked fucked fucked* head, slap herself
silly until she feels absolutely nothing at all. But even that will not
help.

She pulls out her journal and grabs a pen and lets her raw
anguish gush out onto the page like blood from a freshly opened
wound.

SIMON

And then it's the weirdest thing, because snake-eyes Simon keeps buzzing around her.

Even at the Club. This is new. The other kids think it's kind of strange. Robbing the cradle, for one thing. Even in this group, certain boundaries seem to apply.

Then Cal starts acting funny, all threatened, swaggering when he's around Simon like some dominant male animal, making sure his half-erect cock shows through his painted-on jeans. It's nuts.

Mallory feels almost popular. She is not sure she trusts the feeling and knows it won't last.

She doesn't know what she thinks about Simon, but it has changed since they had that little talk.

She thinks he's sexy and magnetic in a frightening kind of way. She's still a little scared of him. All those tattoos. But he's smarter than he seems, and smarter than Cal by a long shot. Though sometimes Mallory thinks tree lichen would be smarter than Cal.

She has wondered about Annie's baby, of course, could it really be Simon's, because they were sort of hanging out, going around together for a while. Annie started Simon going to the Rev, and Simon's influence has slowly dragged the rest of the group over to the church, out of curiosity if nothing else.

And Annie's much more his type, tall and tanned and young and lovely, while Mallory's dark and small and unsettlingly boyish. Though she's gone up a bra size, all the way up to 34A, with only a little Kleenex stuffed in the front, and taken to removing her glasses to speak to people. Then they get to look into those simmering, level blue eyes full-force.

She starts showing Simon bits of her novel, and some of the comments he makes are pretty astute. Even some of the criticisms.

He's right on about a lot of things. Then he gets a fucking brilliant idea: could he do some illustrations?

The thought of the two of them pouring their energies together makes Mallory want to swoon with excitement.

When he shows her a pen and ink drawing of Maid Madeleine's steed, Silvernor, rearing up on his hind legs, she feels almost faint. This is exactly the way she pictured him, a supernaturally powerful creature with flame spurting out of his nostrils. And Madeleine: that's it, that's her creation! How did he know exactly what she wanted, that certain kind of sad serenity? She and Simon will be a team, they'll publish books together, they'll be best-sellers, Simon's art will be famous and Mallory will win the Pulitzer Prize, or at least the Governor General's award for literature. They'll get married and live in a loft in Montreal, no, Paris. (Wait a minute. *Married?*) Mallory tries on his last name. Mallory . . . Sarkisian? No, it doesn't sound quite right. Maybe she'll keep Mardling as her professional name?

She's pretty sure something is going to happen and when it starts to, when he touches the back of her neck with a certain near-tenderness, then lifts up her now-longish dark hair and kisses the nape of her neck, she is not completely surprised. Yet terrified.

They're standing there in Gail's bedroom where kids go to be alone, make out and things. Mostly talk.

"Uh, Simon . . ."

"C'mon, Mallie. Don't be so scared."

"I just don't know if I'm ready to . . ."

"I won't do anything you don't want." He slides one hand very gently into her blouse and cups her left breast. Mallory thinks her body is going to explode.

She can feel her face darkening with blood. He leans forward to give her the lightest, most grazing kiss, and it is all she can do to forcibly restrain herself from leaping on him. He keeps on kissing, so lightly, no tongue, just soft lips exploring. Mallory realizes she loves kissing, if the boy does it right. Cal went too fast. Simon opens his mouth a little and so does she.

Lightning strikes from below, flashing upwards. Every nerve in her body is illuminated. A great groaning beanstalk sprouts between her legs and slowly lifts her up off the ground and into the sky.

"I'd like to touch you," Simon says.

"You are touching me."

"I mean with no clothes on."

"Shit. Simon, I don't know about this."

"I think you want me to do this."

She can't argue.

"And I won't put myself inside you. I don't think you're ready for that."

"Yeah, but don't boys sort of like go crazy and do stuff they can't control?" Mallory realizes she sounds like her IQ has plummeted by at least fifty points. Simon smiles and starts to unbutton her blouse. No haste.

Mallory is turning all dappley where he touches her. Pink and mottled. When he takes her bra off with surprisingly little fumbling, her nipples look like twin raspberries. He takes one in his mouth and sucks gently, tonguing her.

Mallory gasps. Her head snaps backward and tears form in her eyes, involuntary tears of too much pleasure.

"Okay?" he murmurs, looking concerned.

"Yes. I'm fine. I'm just not used to it."

"I'll go slow."

He takes forever. He covers her body in small, close kisses, a dense, lush carpet of flowers. Mallory realizes that she has never felt precisely like this before. Usually a surge of sexual desire makes her want to get herself off quickly. This is different, slower, infinitely more huge, and her body swells as if it is being gradually filled with helium.

He works his way deliberately down. Undoes her white shorts, and then she panics. God! He's going to see it. He's going to see it.

"What's happening?"

"Simon, I . . . maybe we better stop."

"Does it feel good?"

"Of course it feels good. It's just . . . I look sort of . . . I'm sort of different."

"I know."

"*What?*"

"Gail said."

"Oh, Christ."

"Don't worry about it. I won't hurt you."

By this time, she believes him.

"I just don't want you freaking out," she says, a little choked up. He continues pulling her shorts off, then her pink cotton panties. He tenderly touches her bush, and she can't believe how the pleasure keeps on escalating.

When she is sure the experience can't get any better, it does. It *insists*: some force a thousand times more powerful than either one of them has swallowed them whole. Mallory wonders for the hundredth time why all this is considered so dirty, so wrong. To her it feels like a kind of miracle.

He parts her legs and looks at her carefully. As if examining or peering on some wonder.

"Looks like an Easter egg," he says with amusement in his voice.

"That's a new one." She starts to pull away.

"No, I mean it. A little pink Easter egg with fluffy Easter grass all around it."

"You don't think I'm a fucking freak?"

"It's just a clit. I think it's kind of pretty." He begins to kiss all around it and Mallory realizes she won't be able to stop herself, if he keeps on doing what he is doing she will come all over his face.

And he keeps on doing what he is doing.

And then—

Then his soft gentle tongue touches her Easter egg, and in a few seconds the orgasm she has been holding back by main strength rips through her entire being with a wild will of its own. She bites her fist to keep from crying out.

Simon watches her, his eyes shining.

"Jesus," she says.

"It's good, isn't it?"

"Yes . . . yes, you might say that."

"Didn't hurt?"

"Christ, no."

"Good."

"It felt . . . it felt amazing. Why is this considered so wrong?"

"I don't know. Too much power to play with, I guess."

"But you didn't get anything out of it."

"I can get myself off later. No worries. I think you've had about all you can handle for one day."

"God, Simon."

"Don't mention it." He smooths out her panties and gives them back to her. She gets dressed again while he watches.

Then she looks up at him.

"Did we just have sex?"

"I guess so. Something sure happened."

"Am I still a virgin?"

"I'm not sure."

"But I'm not, like, your girlfriend."

"I don't know. Let's not put a label on it."

"Okay."

And they walk downstairs to the rec room glowing, making all the other kids wonder exactly what the hell went on up there.

MARRIED

Mallory wonders what happens when you get married.

Because it seems to her that the married couples she sees don't feel the kind of nearly unbearable, soul-changing pleasure she experienced with Simon.

It seems to her the sexual enchantment goes dead at a certain point. Like, almost right away?

She wonders how it can happen. Something so powerful, so potentially transporting. When you're married, it frees you up to do anything you want with each other, at any time. You can kiss and lick and suck and feel and graze and grab and nuzzle and squeeze to your heart's content.

Why, then, does it die?

Do people get bored? Mallory watches her parents together and it's all milk and newspapers and who takes out the garbage, chores chores chores, no spark any more. She cannot even imagine them having sex, let alone being tender with each other the way Simon was tender with her.

It freaks her out to think about it, yet she can't help thinking about it because here they are with three kids, and as far as she knows they weren't conceived the way Mary supposedly conceived Jesus, from the timely visit of a supernatural being. They fucked each other in the usual old-fashioned way, and Mum got pregnant three different times, so they must have done it more than once.

But now. All these years later when they are no longer in the babymaking business, do they still feel any kind of desire for each other? Mallory needs to know.

Mum has a big solid middle-aged body that has nothing sexy about it, doughy breasts and a stolid, unbendable middle. She wears unsexy print housedresses and flat-heeled shoes. Once in a while she'll put on a dab of red lipstick, a real concession to glamour.

Dad is even worse. Lumpish, graceless, often drunk from the nips he takes out in the little room behind the kitchen where he keeps the private stash of booze he thinks nobody else knows about.

Sex dies. Then what hope is there? And when will it die for her—when she gets married? Does she even want to be married, ever?

She wants to talk about what happened between her and Simon, because even though it would probably sound unbelievably dirty, she feels it was a sort of miracle. There's no one she can talk to about this. Annie isn't even around these days, and she'd be jealous anyway because she and Simon were sort of going out for a while. Mallory wonders if Annie's parents have sent her away or what. There are only two weeks left in the school year and she was all set to start her counselling job, preg or not. You have to hand it to Annie—she does have some nerve.

She can't talk to Dr. Rubens. Not about this. Although it would at least reassure her that she's not a Sapphire or whatever the term she uses is. (It means lesbian, anyway. Would her life be simpler if she were?)

Even writing in her journal about it is difficult. The words won't fashion themselves, won't obey her the way they usually do. She's friendly with Simon still and it's cool, but they haven't made out again and it's plain she isn't his real girlfriend.

It was an Experience, powerful beyond her ability to describe, yet nobody else gets the significance of it. In fact, they'd probably be horrified to hear that she allowed a boy to do that to her.

But it was so *good*. And unlike Annie, she didn't get preg. He didn't do anything to her that she didn't want him to do.

She wants to pray, but doesn't know how. And does God think sex is dirty, too?

Is God just as bad as everybody else? Will God judge her as harshly as her fellow humans, or worse?

But what exactly did she do that was so terrible?

Didn't God make sex? If God didn't, who did? The devil? Is there such a being? Is the flesh really evil? Then why do we consider death so bad? Why don't we welcome it?

The loneliness and confusion of being Mallory are sometimes almost more than she can endure. She sends something up to God, whatever she can, hoping whatever-It-is will hear her, and, in Its tender and infinite mercy, answer.

THE NOVEL

The last week of classes seems to last approximately eighty-seven years.

She feels as if she has popped a corset, or is about to be let out of a cage. Soon she will be able to breathe again after an interminable period of suffocation.

She is a racehorse in the starting gate of summer.

So this is her last chance to show the first seven chapters of *Silvernor* to Mr. Livingston.

Cal said Livingston loves her. Mallory wonders. She even talks to Rubens about it, and her drawn-on black eyebrows shoot up into her hairline.

"He ees interested in your vork?"

"He told me I have the seeds of greatness in me."

"Really."

Seeds of greatness. More than a young girl can handle, obviously. Dr. Rubens writes a single word on Mallory's chart: "Infatuation."

But isn't it normal for a young girl, a bright young girl, a lonely bright young girl, a lonely unusually bright young girl like Mallory to develop a crush on her English teacher?

Mallory hands the first seven chapters of *The Secret of Silvernor* to Mr. Livingston, seventy-five pristine pages typewritten on white bond, along with a sheaf of illustrations by Simon S. Sarkisian Jr. Mallory thinks they're goddamn amazing.

"A novel. Mallory. This is—well, it's more than I expected. It's certainly ambitious of you."

Mr. Livingston shuffles through the pile of drawings, peering at them over his glasses, which have slipped down his greasy long nose.

"They look sort of …"

Brilliant? Inspired? Fucking magnificent?

"They're sort of hippie-looking."

Mallory is stunned.

"Hippie-looking?"

"Don't get me wrong. I think this young man definitely has quite a bit of raw talent. It's a pity he dropped out of school so young, or he could have had a chance to develop it properly."

"What's wrong with them?"

"Now don't be defensive, Mallory. The life of the artist demands that you learn how to handle criticism. You need to use it to improve yourself, to hone your skills."

This is such bullshit. She wishes she hadn't even shown it to him. But now his eyes are boring into her prologue with the same acid, squinched-up, disapproving look.

He doesn't say anything for five, six, seven pages. Mallory's guts writhe. If he hates it, she will die. No, fuck him. What does he know? She'll send it to Random House and they'll give her a fat advance, take out a movie option. She wants Vanessa Redgrave to play Maid Madeleine. Mallory loved her as Guinevere in *Camelot*, her sad, serene face was perfect for the part.

"Really, Mallory, this is … well, it's an interesting premise, but for an apprentice writer such as yourself, shouldn't you set your sights a little bit lower? Once you've mastered the short story …"

"Fuck short stories."

"Mallory!"

"So you hate it. Now what am I supposed to do?" She's close to tears and hates herself for it. She wanted to be cool, no matter what. Now she's dying for a cigarette or something stronger. She rehearses in her head what she will say to the kids tonight. She'll replay the scene in all its shitty glory, just to show them what an asshole Livingston is. As if they don't already know.

"Mallory, I never once said I hated it. Don't read in things I haven't even told you. It's just that the scope … well, it's far too ambitious for a junior writer like you, an ancient fantasy tale that is obviously meant to represent the present day. Even Tolkien wasn't accepted right away, and you do want people to read this, don't you? And the voice of that narrator, the old storyteller—Mallory, what have you been reading?"

"You think I stole it!"

"Settle down, young lady."

"You think I fucking *stole* my story idea."

"Mallory. If you continue to use language like that with me, I'll have to report you to Mr. Crofton."

"Oh, you'll sic Wilbur on me, will you? I'm real scared." But she is scared. Terrified. Her life is sinking. A great sucking hole has opened in the floor of her abdomen and is pulling her guts down and through and out onto the floor.

"Mallory, don't give up on the novel as a form. Perhaps you can return to it later. This is a good attempt. Really, it is. It was brave of you to even try."

Then she realizes something.

She sees it, clear as a laser.

"How many novels have you written, Mr. Livingston?"

"Mallory. That's uncalled-for."

"I mean, how many novels have you *started?* How many novels have you started and never fucking finished because you're just too piss-ass to continue? How many times did you have to try writing novels to find out you have no fucking *talent*, and that's why you're a goddamn high school English teacher instead of a *writer?*"

A crackling, hissing silence. The air pops with rage.

Then, something Mallory never even counted on.

Mr. Livingston—Kenneth—Ken—Kenny—begins to cry. He's pretending not to, like men always do (*chickenshit bastards*, Mallory thinks, her brain seething), but he really truly is crying and can't hold it back any more because Mallory has scored a direct hit.

For one poisonous instant he stands naked, stripped, his life a total sham.

Mallory is horrified, horrified at what she has done. She wants to put her arms around him, to apologize profusely, but can't. She gathers up the pile of papers in her arms, shaking. Mr. Livingston turns away and clears his throat.

"As a warning," he says.

What?

"As a warning. One more profane outburst like that, Miss Mardling, and I will report you, not to Wilbur Crofton but to Principal McGuinness. You're well aware that the penalty for using such obscene and filthy language in front of a teacher is immediate and permanent expulsion. How would you like that, Mallory? Would you like to be expelled?"

Mallory is beginning to think it would be heaven on earth.

But there is always her career to consider. To have her education derailed now would probably hold her back.

And she would miss the kids.

And she would catch hell from her parents, and have to stay home with Victor all the time.

"No, Mr. Livingston, I would not."

"A warning, then." He has forced back the tears successfully and is no longer vulnerable. Emotion is the enemy, apparently. Mallory wonders how you can win this battle, so life-hating. She wonders how it started, how he got the idea he was not allowed to feel.

She hates him and at the same time she wants to touch him, wants to touch his face where the hard battened-down lines have suddenly appeared, the lines of repression. She remembers the poem about the Tin Man, and wonders if Mr. Livingston ever longs to have a heart.

"I'm sorry." She means this. She hopes he sees that. "It's just that I worked on this for so long, and I hoped . . ."

"You hoped. I hoped. We all hoped." He's not making much sense any more, and it scares her.

"Yes, I hoped. I thought that's what you wanted me to do."

He takes off his glasses and rubs his pouchy red eyes, looking terribly threadbare and middle-aged. Mallory wonders why people become so ugly when they get old. And what is that smell about him, that stale something—is it failed dreams?

"Mallory, you have talent, there's no disputing that fact. But you're fourteen years old. What do you know about the world? A novel. Whew!"

"I'm going to finish it."

He looks at her with a flicker of admiration. "I'll bet you will."

"I'll have it finished by September."

"Mallory . . ."

"I can't come on your sailboat with you, Kenneth."

"Take my home phone number, at least."

"I'll be busy. Busy writing."

"As you wish." He pulls himself together, puts on his best teacherly smile. "And good luck to you, Mallory."

"Thank you, sir."

The sir part just slipped out.

Then she takes her manuscript into the girls' washroom, slams the door of the cubicle, bashes her head ten times on the hard metal wall, sits down on the can and bawls until she wants to throw up.

ANNIE GONE

Annie is gone, and of course the kids have noticed it.

What happened to her summer job? It went to somebody else. Have they sent her away?

They send girls away. Everybody has a story. They come back changed, sober and quiet. Broken. Or your parents make you have an abortion, the foetus ripped out of your body in agony, probably with a coat hanger, and then you can't have children any more ever, or you "have to get married" and it's miserable, and you hate each other forever and the baby grows up warped. A whole lot of fatal choices. Are there any good choices when you're pregnant and don't want the kid?

The talk burbles on and on at various levels, as if she had this coming, she was a slut anyway, she fucked everything in sight and didn't use precautions. But when a small article appears in the *Kennewick Standard*, the story erupts, blooming luridly into a tragedy ready to happen.

LOCAL GIRL DISAPPEARS. Mr. and Mrs. Voortman tell the press that Annie was a happy girl, attractive, well-adjusted, popular, not on drugs like some of these kids who grow up with no supervision, oh no, she's a good girl, raised in the Church. (Which means no sex. Church and sex are mutually exclusive.) She must have run away. Hitchhiked to Thunder Bay or something. But how will she survive? Mallory hopes she does not resort to selling her particular skills. She once listened slack-jawed as Annie described to her in minute detail how to perform a blow job. Mallory wonders how someone so young could have learned this. She wonders why anyone would ever want to do such a thing. The idea of having a man's dick in her mouth disgusts her, it must taste like pee or something, but apparently men love this, all men, queer, straight or in-between, old and young alike. And are willing to pay for the favour because, for the most part, their wives won't cooperate. No wonder. The act must be about as pleasant for them as taking out the garbage or cleaning toilets.

Marriage tames sex, renders it harmless, ruins it. Yet what to do with sex? It is a wild animal, a polecat waiting to spray. The source of all things and therefore infinitely mysterious, yet also a thing of jism and stinks and groans and disease and babies nobody wants. And look what it did to Annie. She is out there somewhere, surely?

Then Mallory thinks of the Rev.

Summer is hanging around now like mist, like a sultry smell, and the Rev's group, now burgeoning with kids, is winding down, though there is supposed to be some sort of a barbecue in Kennewick Park in July. (*Weenies for Jesus,* Simon calls it.) The Rev is putting out a certain kind of sweat, a gin-exuding anxiety that is almost palpable, or at least it's palpable to Mallory, whose antennae are out there so far they make her look like a Martian.

Surely not. Could he be so bad? Is the Rev good? What does his congregation think of him? Are people beginning to suspect something? Are any of the kids talking about what happens? A confetti of questions, blizzard-like and confusing. One thing Mallory knows. He is addictive. No one can get enough of him, uncomfortable as his overpowering presence sometimes is. He is doing baptisms now and Mallory is relieved he doesn't use a murky tank of water like the Baptists, but there's none of that feeble shaking-on of droplets, either, he uses a big glass pitcher that Simon says ought to have a Kool-Aid face painted on the side. Since everybody seems to have really long hair now except Mallory, there's a lot of dripping and streaming and sobbing, and rising up new. Mallory wishes she could rise up new, or at least rise up without feeling wretched in the morning, the grey funk of depression sealing off her air. She holds back on being baptized, even though she's practically the only kid who won't go through with the experience. Simon won't, either, he's a little too smart for that.

They're sitting in the rec room in Gail's aunt's house, talking. Since their encounter, Mallory feels something for him that she can't quite define, a small warm spot that makes the ache in the rest of her almost unbearable.

"Kenny didn't like the novel."

"What about the pictures?"

"Said they were hippie-looking."

"Well, fuck him then. He's an asshole anyway. Child-molester, practically."

"He hasn't tried anything."

"Yet. Don't go on his sailboat, Mallory. He probably has a bed all set up below deck."

"I think he just likes me."

"You kidding? You scare him half to death."

This pleases Mallory, but she tries to hide her smile. And she's not entirely pleased to be pleased.

"Hey, Simon?"

"Yeah."

"What d'you think happened to Annie?"

"Maybe she went to Toronto."

"God, I hope not."

"Why? That's where we should be."

"You mean—where we'd be appreciated?"

"Where there's some sort of a fucking future. This place is a complete dead end."

Comfy, cozy Kennewick, home of frustrated teenagers, perverted Reverends and runaway blondes.

"Are you thinking of leaving?"

"I've left already. Just waiting for my chance."

"I'd miss you." Mallory generally does not allow herself to be this naked in front of anyone. But he has tasted her, for God's sake, made her come electric. Why is it so difficult to make this small confession?

"Come with me."

Mallory knows she can't.

"Come on."

"I'm not ready. I'm fourteen, for Christ's sake."

"So, I'm seventeen. Big fat hairy deal. It's just a number."

But Mallory knows she can't. Can't say why, either. She's afraid, but that's not really the reason. Something to do with Annie? Someone has to care enough about her to find out just what the hell happened to her, where she is. Girls get killed on the road. Or damaged so badly they want to be dead. She may look eighteen, but she's only fourteen, like Mallory, they have almost the same birthday in February, and no matter how many blow jobs she's done, she is shockingly naïve, with no equipment to deal with life.

No sense of what some men are capable of. Men who have lost some vital part of themselves, hollow men, their compassion rusted away to holes.

Sometimes I think I've got to get out. Got to get out of Kennewick, just go with Simon, take off somewhere, anywhere. Or go alone. Like Annie?

It's all such shit.

Victor plays with himself right in front of me now. In spite of all the pills, in spite of all the shrinks, he's not getting any better. In fact, he keeps on going deeper into weirdness, a weirdness that only makes sense to him. My parents know nothing, just nothing, about anything that matters.

"So how has it been going with Dr. Rubens, Mallory?"

"Oh, just fine, Mum."

"Is she helping you adjust at school?"

"Yeah."

"Are you sure you're being honest with me, Mallory?"

Since when has Mum ever really wanted me to be honest about anything?

She acts strange now, cries at funny times, maybe because of Gramma being dead, who knows. Mum is really, really old. She had me late, a "surprise." When you're 43 you don't expect another baby, don't want one. So I have a Mum who looks more like a grandmother. It's embarrassing. But the same thing must've happened to her mum, because Gramma was nearly 100 years old when she finally died.

Sometimes I feel her, around. And it's nice. I wonder if she is protecting me.

If I went, then, would I be okay?

And where would I go?

I want to nail the Rev. Nail him in his lie. He knows something about Annie. I don't want to think he is capable of what I am starting to suspect.

But I have to find out. Maybe he's just like Kenny, a bastard on the outside and mush inside. Weak.

I could look for her. I know where she likes to hang out. Fuck school. There's hardly any time left anyway, only a couple of days, and fuck the yearbook, even with my essay in it. Though I've dreamed about it all my life, getting published will only pull down my popularity another notch, as if such a thing were possible.

Yesterday Dr. Rubens asks me what I'm going to do during my summer vacation. Such an original question.

"Finish my novel," I tell her.

"And do you haf any social plans?"

Social plans. Take off to Toronto with Simon? Go underground, undercover, find my runaway friend?

"I figured I'd join the 4-H Club."

"Yes. And zis—4-H Club, vhat is its purpose?"

Oh, it's too easy with her, too easy to just diddle her around. Grown-ups are such idiots.

"They show prize bulls and stuff. Raise pigs and win blue ribbons."

"Mallory. Zis is not your area."

So what *is* my area? Looking under rocks? Trying to get below the bullshit I'm buried in and get at the truth?

"My friend is gone." All of a sudden I feel like crying.

"Ah. Anika Voortman."

"You've heard?" I'm freaking amazed.

"You haf spoken of zis Annie. And I do read ze paper."

Maybe Dr. Rubens is not as stupid as she looks. I can see by the look on her face that she's concerned about Annie.

And if she's concerned about Annie, is it possible she's also concerned about me? I mean, it's her job to talk to me, she has no choice in the matter, but this is the first time I've considered the possibility that in spite of all that, she might actually care.

So I decide to take a big fat risk and tell her the truth.

"She's pregnant."

Dr. Rubens's eyes fly open with shock.

"How do you know zis?"

"She told me in the bathroom."

(Things said in the bathroom are always true. It's like a confessional in porcelain.)

"But she iss fourteen."

"Last time I checked you could get knocked up at fourteen."

"Are you vorried?"

"She could be dead. Or out on the street somewhere. Yeah, I worry."

"Your church. Could zey help? Do you pr-rey for her?"

I'd pray, yes, sure, if I had any fucking clue who or what I was praying to, if I had any idea at all who or what is out there, if such an entity even exists, and if so, if He, She or It would listen to me and bother to do anything about it.

"Sometimes I question the value of prayer."

"It can be a source of str-rength."

"Really, Dr. Rubens. I thought you Freudians were all atheists."

"Not necessarily."

"But what is prayer? It's basically telling God what to do. Hi there, God, it's me, Mallory Mardling. And I'm here to tell you what you should be doing to run the universe according to my own dearest wishes and desires. Of course, to ask you any of this, I have to assume that I know better than you do."

Dr. Rubens is trying not to smile.

"Mallory, how cynical."

"But it's true! God, do this! God, do that! It's nuts. I'm this particle of humanity, this speck among billions, and I'm expecting *God* to turn the whole world the other way because that's what I personally happen to desire? And what if fifty other people are praying for the opposite of what I'm asking for? Who does God listen to? Does he draw straws or something?"

Dr. Rubens has no idea what to say.

And then I go home that night and I get down beside my bed like I'm seven years old again.

Because I'm so fucking scared for Annie, so scared that I'd do just about anything, even try to boss the head of the whole universe, just on the off chance that He, She or It will intervene.

THE LETTER

And then.

It's like an answered prayer, the letter.

Enough to make her feel, at least for the moment, that He/She/It cares about her, and maybe even about Annie too.

It flutters down through the mail slot in the door, on baby-pink stationery in hot-pink ink, along with a couple of rejection slips from *Pegasus* and *Windborne* magazines.

It's on a round piece of paper, written in a circle, so Mallory has to keep turning, and turning, and turning.

> MALLORY!!!
>
> It's freaking amazing what's been happening to me!! Blows my mind. I've got my own apartment now! It is so *cool*. And I've met this neat bunch of kids. I'm working at a boutique in town selling the coolest clothes. And my parents don't even care! I think they're glad to get rid of me.
>
> I even have a new boyfriend named Wesley. God, you've just *got* to come see me so you can meet him! Why don't you just take off? Pack a few things and hitch, or take the bus. Comstock isn't that far, not really, and it's way cooler than Kennewick! Come see me, eh? Love ya! (kiss, kiss, kiss)—Annie. P.S. Don't you DARE tell anyone else where I am, *on pain of death*!!

There's an address in Comstock, with an apartment number and everything. The postmark checks out. Mallory can't remember seeing Annie's handwriting before, but who else could have sent this?

And the timing couldn't be more perfect. Mum and Dad are away in Toronto at a conference for Dad's work. Something to do with stationery and school supplies. They'll be gone for three weeks, because they want to turn it into a little holiday. All this trouble with Victor, and now Mallory, then Gramma dying, they deserve to get away for a little while to relax. Nola says she'll keep an eye on things, then promptly takes off with her thirty-year-old boyfriend Andrew.

So Mallory and Victor are left alone.

Victor, who, like Tommy in the rock opera about the pinball wizard, doesn't know what day it is, just sits around in the puddle of his ruined mind, marinating in his own rank juices.

"See you later, Victor. I'm going away for a few days." Mallory has a small bag packed and has bought a Greyhound ticket to Comstock. She has taken $150.00 out of her savings account, full of baby bonus cheques and Gramma's wrinkly old dollar bills, carefully hoarded for some future emergency.

"Hey, sis." At least Victor still speaks English. He drifts in and out of clarity like a radio with several vital wires pulled.

"What?"

"You aren't too happy, are you."

"Happy?"

"I've seen you. I hear you crying, too. I know you're going to a shrink."

"And you're not?"

"Yeah, but I'm s'posed to be nuts."

"Maybe I am too."

"Doubt it. Just fucked-up. You wanna smoke?"

"Don't have time. I have to go see my friend."

"That Annie?"

"I didn't know you knew about Annie."

"I'm crazy, not stupid."

"So what have you heard?

"She got knocked up, ran away. Maybe Toronto. Her stepfather fucked her up pretty good."

Mallory is astonished.

"How in hell did you know about the stepfather?"

"I get out sometimes."

Yes, Mallory thinks, when he is well enough to make a little sense. The rest of the time he exudes mental illness like a wild high reek, a skunk cloud that surrounds his body with a nearly visible social barricade.

"Who've you been talking to?"

"I know Simon. We have the same dealer."

Mallory's gut clenches. *Oh crap. What else does he—?*

"Do you know about the Rev?"

"A little. Get out of that shit, Mallory. It's bad religion. You're way too smart to fall for that stuff."

"I can think for myself."

"Simon says he's got everyone nearly brainwashed."

"Not everyone." She gathers up her stuff, slings the big tooled leather bag over her shoulder.

"Hey, sis. Don't get raped or anything."

"Girls who look like boys don't get raped."

"That's how much you know. *Boys* get ass-fucked all the time. Happened to me in the hospital."

"Christ." She wants to feel sympathy for him, but since he popped a mainspring he looks so scary, almost demonic, and it's off-putting, like Gramma's pruned ancient body curved into a dessicated C.

She wants to remember him as he was, funny, fiercely smart, melting lead over the Bunsen burner and making shapes, playing the guitar and singing better than Gordon Lightfoot, causing the girls to sigh.

Things change. That's all she knows. They don't change in a good way, either. She wonders about Annie's baby, whether she got rid of it or not. She didn't say anything in the letter. Or is she going to hook up with this Wesley guy and try to raise the baby herself? Her boutique job sounds a little suspicious. Too good to be true. Maybe she's dealing dope or something, or using some of her other skills.

Mallory sits on the Greyhound for an hour and forty-five minutes, brooding over Annie, trying to filter out the stink of human bodies all around her. Sometimes she wonders, pressed close to other people, how they can stand to smell so bad. Like unwashed genitals, like an unwiped bum, like the pissy old armpit of an unlaundered sweater. Rancid scalps, shitty breath and stale, fungal feet.

The people around her exude poverty and failure. They all seem to have pimples and bad clothes, many of them are fat and misshapen, most wear a furrowed, sagging expression. The flesh almost seems to hang from their faces. Mallory wonders for the hundredth time why misfortune manifests itself in such a dense cluster: no money, bad looks, defeated manner. Then there are the Golden Ones, sunny of hair, clear of eye, bonny to look at, smelling fresh, and with plenty of fresh-smelling banknotes crackling away in their wallets. God must love them more than all the rest of us, she surmises, to grant them that many favours.

She knows she's not one of the Golden Ones and never will be. She's one of the bus people. Downtrodden. Riding the loser cruiser all the way through to oblivion.

Except she has a destination, the little town of Comstock, duller than Kennewick by half. Or at least smaller. Dingier, too, she notices when she gets off the bus.

Everything seems to be tinged with grey, even people's faces.

She tries to imagine them having sex, and can't. It is surprising how few people she can imagine having sex.

She doesn't know one end of Comstock from another—not that there's much to know. But she doesn't want to spend all day wandering around, trying to find Winterson Avenue. It probably looks like every other dull old avenue or dull old street in this nothing of a place. So she hails a cab, probably the only taxi in all of Comstock, and shells out a few precious dollars of her getaway money to take her to Annie's place.

The address she gave isn't far. Nothing would be. The ancient cabbie, his wattle of a face as red as if it's been boiled, voice

painful as walking barefoot on gravel, takes her money and lets
her off at the corner of Winterson and Greenwald.

1857 Winterson Avenue, Apartment #19. The cab has already
pulled away when Mallory realizes the numbers are all wrong.

Or something is. There is a long stretch of what looks like
industrial park, with no numbers on the buildings at all.

She looks at the address again.

Could Annie have written it wrong?

Where her apartment should be, something is either being
torn down or built up, Mallory can't decide which. Broken glass
sparkling on the ground, brown corpses of spent beer bottles, bad
damp smells of things that have soured. But no one is there. No
construction crew, or destruction crew, or anything.

Almost no one.

For when she steps across the threshold of the ruined place,
she feels a quick electrical rising of the pollen-soft hairs on her
face. From behind her the air chills ever so slightly as the black
shape of blotted-out light drops over her head.

Her gut has no time to leap.

RUBBER

She can still smell things.

Urinous smells like a man whose clothes are not very clean, and rubber, but that would be the big thing he has just shoved into her mouth.

For it has to be a man. No woman's hands would smell like that, like malt and salt and overcooked molasses.

First there is the strange sensation of moving backwards by force, her arms wrenched hard behind her back. Then blankness, not blackness exactly but something hampering her head, a fabric wound around her face so that her eyes are completely covered. The cloth has a rancid, ant-trap odour and a greasy feel, like an unwashed tablecloth. The rubber thing between her teeth nearly makes her gag, a bit forced into the mouth of a horse, bringing a flood of nauseated saliva.

She staggers forward for several steps, pushed by the rough, smelly hands. Then her head is shoved down and under. There are more smells, a flood of them, as if her sense of smell has grown huge to compensate for the blindness, the distasteful reek of a smoke-soaked automobile tarred with gaseous layers of nicotine.

A lurch forward, and they're driving fast. Another shove, and her head is pushed down hard and out of sight.

She must be in the back, so no one will see her.

She wonders if anyone will ever see her again. The feeling is below fear, in that place of *extremis* where simple enduring is the only choice, where a strange presence inside her head keeps saying, "It's not that bad, it's not that bad," while instinct shrieks that death is imminent.

Mallory's heart bashes dangerously against the walls of her

chest, her knees forced upwards into her chin, her tongue squeezed bloody by the gag. They drive and drive.

That's it, my life is over. Fuck, I'm going to die now without finishing the novel. Without testing sex, without even finding out if I like it. Without discovering how it feels to love a man deeply. Without ever seeing my friends again. Without my name on a book. Everything is going to stop now, all of it, all I've ever known, just stop.

If there's a Christ, make this unhappen. Make it stop, God, if there is one. I will never doubt you again if you will just let me Jesusly GO.

THE BOX

She is inside a box, or something like it. A small and stuffy space, all sound muffled and enclosed. The air is dense with a closet staleness.

Her captor's fingers remind her of sausages, vaguely greasy and smelling of rendered fat. She hates the feel of them peeling off the mask of cloth over her eyes, dredging out the gag. He leaves her hands tied behind her back.

"Where the fuck *am* I?" The shriek escapes her mouth before she can stop it from flying out.

"Shut up. I'm not gonna hurt you."

She has heard that voice before. She knows it. But the face? Christ, it's only a kid. Some fucking teenager, for God's sake. How could such a pimply little weasel mastermind all this, plan it out, lie in wait?

"I want to know where I am."

"Promise me you won't scream again."

"What good would it do?"

"I already said I'm not gonna hurt you."

"Yeah? Like, I'm supposed to trust you? Who *are* you? Why've you done this? Where am I?" The light is a washy grey in this suffocating little box, filtered daylight through a dirty half-window—so she must be in a basement. The air feels damp and subterranean. Mallory can make out the shape of an army cot in the corner. The rest of the tiny room is piled with broken junk, boxes of stuff, wheels from a boy's bicycle, a lamp shade, an unstrung lacrosse stick, painty old clothes in a heap, a dog carrier and an old TV.

The boy grabs her shoulders and forces her down on the crummy little cot. His touch makes her quail.

"If you do everything I tell you, you won't get hurt."

Then she knows where she has heard that voice before.

The church.

She strains to remember the face.

"This has something to do with Annie," Mallory says, then wishes she hadn't, for the savage backhanded whack in the face takes her completely by surprise, exploding across her eyes and nose with nauseating force.

I thought he said he wasn't going to hurt me, a small voice inside Mallory says.

Shut up. Shut up. We've got to get out of this.

I'm scared. I don't know where I am. I might get raped.

Shut up! Watch him. Figure him out. He's just a kid. We can do this.

"I have to pee," she says.

The kid looks completely disconcerted. It's not what he expected her to say, especially not after just whacking her.

"Tough shit."

"Come on. You can't just hold me here forever without letting me go to the bathroom."

"Jesus." He grabs her arm and yanks her up, through the doorway and into a place blacker than hell, a place where bats might hang upside down all day. He drags her towards a crack of light, another little room that must be a bathroom, but she wrenches away and throws her body at a small seep of light that turns out to be the bottom of a staircase. She is flinging herself at it, scrambling desperately upwards, when she feels her feet being grabbed and yanked.

Her skull lands on cement with an alarming *crack*, followed by cold blankness like sinking into heavy sleep.

VOICES

We have to get out of here.

Mum. I want my Mum.

Shut up. Christ, we're tied to the goddamn bed now. I can't see anything. Is it after dark?

I'm going to die. I'll die in here and no one will ever know where I am.

The kid has to come back. He wouldn't just leave us here. You know how these things go. They bring food and stuff. The whole idea is to keep us alive, or he would've just killed us by now.

My head hurts.

Don't think about it. This has something to do with Annie. Otherwise he wouldn't have freaked out like that. It was a set-up.

I'm hungry. And I have to pee.

If this has something to do with Annie, then it has something to do with the Rev.

I don't want to die.

You're not going to die. You're smarter than this dumb fuck. And you're way smarter than the Rev. He's half cracked or he wouldn't have done anything this stupid. God knows what he's done with Annie.

He killed her.

We can't think about that now.

(This much she knows: there are two of her now, so she must be going mad. One of her, the one who can still think, sees into the future. A vision of her waxen body dumped in the Kennewick River. Or buried under a house. The baby stopped, all life winked out. The colour of death is not black, like this room, or red like gore, but pale blue, translucent. A harmless, infant colour. And powerless.)

VICTOR

Days pass before Victor realizes Mallory is gone.

The house becomes increasingly cluttered, then smelly and squalid, piled with old food, dirty pans, stale clothes, live cigarettes tossed, sodden towels thrown down anywhere. He leaves the water running, burners turned on. The reek of pot slowly fills the place.

Mallory's classmates wonder why she isn't in school for the last day. It's yearbook day, one of the coolest days of the year, and Mallory's essay is in there and everything.

She pretended not to care, but everyone knows how much she wants to see it.

Mr. Livingston wonders if he should phone her, then thinks better of it. Her withering comments at their last meeting alarmed him. He feels ashamed that a slip of a girl could have such a devastating effect on him. He is almost afraid of her. But can't let her go.

Simon calls the house. The phone rings seventeen times.

Dr. Rubens crosses out her name in the appointment book. Obviously she is not coming.

In Toronto, Mr. and Mrs. Mardling clink their wineglasses, feeling mellow and relaxed for the first time in what seems like years.

PRAYER

Okay. Here's the deal.

I'm in this place and I can't move. The guy comes around once every hundred years or so to feed me and take me to the bathroom. I guess he doesn't want me doing it in my pants. He never says anything. He's acting like he's looking after somebody's hamster while they're on vacation.

I can hardly see anything because the light is so bad. The little window is way too small to crawl out of, even if I could get my wrists free and find something to smash it with.

That's the deal. Here is where I am. Here is where You, in Your infinite wisdom and mercy, have chosen to put me. Either that, or all this is happening against Your will. And aren't You supposed to be all-powerful: omnipotent, omniscient and omnipresent?

I won't even go into things like Nazi Germany and all that, or even why you made Victor nuts. Let's keep it simple, eh? You're supposed to see the little sparrow fall, etc. The very hairs on my head are numbered. Then *why?* Why am I here? If I die here, what will have been the bloody point?

I could ask You to get me the fuck *out* of this. In fact, I am asking You now. But I have a feeling nothing will happen.

I even think about Mum and Dad. I don't want to, they're jerks, but they keep popping into my head. Sometimes I even say it out loud: *Mum. I want my mum.* I think about Mr. Livingston and the shitty way I treated him when he criticized my novel. The way I made him cry, and just for a minute I had this mean sense of triumph. I think about Dr. Rubens, the way I made horrible fun of her accent to my friends, like she's a Nazi, when she's probably only Dutch or something. Is that why all this is happening, some sort of divine retribution? Are You getting back at me now for being such a shit? Or am I just so bored with not being able to move that my mind is eating itself alive?

I really do want my mum. I just want to see her again, I want to hear her voice, I don't care if she likes me or not. This is like a movie, every bad cliché coming true.

Please! Please!

All right, forget I said that. I won't beg. It won't do me any good. I'm going to get through this whatever way I can. I can last a long time here if he keeps giving me food and water, even if the food is only a baloney sandwich on stale Wonder Bread.

But there has to be a point to this, right? Something to do with the Rev. And Annie. Annie must be dead by now.

That means he is capable of anything.

Christ, if You're there, don't let him do this again. With Annie and the baby, that's two already. Don't let things happen in threes. There's so much stuff I want to do. I didn't realize how badly until now. I just want to live, I don't care how my life turns out or how crappy things are right now, I'm going to write books, I'm going to get out of Kennewick forever. But only if I fucking survive.

Help me fucking survive.

BLINDED

Next time the kid feeds her, he puts the blindfold back on her, and Mallory knows something worse is about to happen.

"Frank, what're you doing?"

"My name's not Frank."

"You won't tell me your name, so I'll call you what I want."

"I'm just following directions."

"That's what the ss said."

"The what?"

"The Nazis, Frank. You know, Adolph Eichmann and the gang. Nobody would take responsibility for anything. They were just following orders."

"Watch your mouth, cunt."

Mallory hasn't been called that in a long time. It's a slap in the face, a hard one.

"I get to talk, for Christ's sake. You want me alive, don't you? If I'm alive, I'm going to talk."

"You'll have a visitor."

Mallory knows who it will be. The blindfold isn't necessary.

"Frank. You're going to get caught. People at the church will figure out what he's doing. They'll find me anyway. Why not let me go now, before something really bad happens?"

"I don't know what you're talking about." Frank heads for the door, and if Mallory weren't tied down she would fling herself at him, wrap herself around his skinny little body, much as she hates him: please, *please* don't leave me alone in this place. But he is gone, and another eon passes in absolute darkness.

Mallory's pulse pounds in her ears.

Then the door cracks open.

It's not Frank. How she can tell, she can't say exactly. Her heart jerks like a hooked perch, and she presses her thighs together so she won't soak herself.

"If you cooperate with me," a voice tells her, "I won't hurt you."

Rage wells in her, overtaking fear.

"Like you're going to let me go now! I know too much. That's why I'm here."

"But I will let you go. I need to explain a few things."

"Then untie me and take this blinder off. Treat me like a human being."

Nothing happens. Is he thinking it over?

Then she feels his hands on her face and has an almost over-whelming urge to bite him, sink her teeth into his flesh until she hits blood. Then the mask of cloth is lifted so she can see again, restoring a shred of sanity and control.

He looks—smaller. Almost a shrunken version of himself. Mallory thought a captor would seem huge, menacing. But he looks hollowed-out, haunted, almost as if he still has the remnants of a conscience.

"Mallory, I think you're overreacting to the situation with Annie. She's perfectly safe. I sent her to Bethesda Centre, a place for young girls who are pregnant out of wedlock. Her parents agreed with me that this was the best plan for her."

And he's a lousy liar. His pupils are contracting.

"Then why am I here?"

"We need to talk some things over. I think it would be best if you went away for a while, too. Just for the summer."

"Where? To camp?"

"I can enroll you in a summer program for gifted students. You can study creative writing. I'd be happy to cover the cost for you."

Mallory stares directly into his eyes and she notices for the first time something saurian about them, too basic, eyes that speak of survival at any cost.

"In exchange for which, I'll shut up."

"Annie's a very troubled young girl, Mallory, from a broken home. She doesn't always tell the truth. I know who the father of her child is."

"So do I."

"I think it's better for everyone concerned if you—"

"Annie's dead, isn't she?"

Mallory sees that his face is beginning to glisten faintly in the dim light of the room.

"You have no proof of that."

"You're in so deep now, you'll do practically anything to save yourself."

"Do you know what you're saying?"

"I know what Annie told me."

"Considering your position, Miss Mardling, I think you should be very careful what you say."

"Once you've killed me, what more can you do to me?"

Mallory watches as he unbuckles his belt. Draws it deliberately out of the loops.

Doubles it in his hand.

Brings it down hard on her body, three times. She can't stop the whimpers of pain and fear, though she hates to show him any signs of weakness.

He beats her systematically, coldly, as if he has a right. She curls and writhes on the cot, electric with pain, nearly crazy with it. By this time she knows she is not dealing with a whole human being.

He stares at her, his eyes brilliant with some sort of pure raw energy, nearly erotic in its intensity.

"Please don't hurt me any more." Her voice shakes, though she tries hard to hold it steady.

He likes this.

He begins to put the belt back on. His face returns to a more normal colour.

But he is not through yet.

He draws closer. A faint smile curls the corners of his mouth. His hands fall on her and she jumps. This is worse than the belt, far worse. His fingers fiddle with the buttons of her blouse. Cold air streams in and her nipples tighten with fear. He draws his hand over her breasts, fondling. Mallory can feel his exhalations on her stomach. She feels weak and sick. She will be raped now. Killed?

"Dolph."

He looks shocked.

"Dolph, I think we have to talk about this."

How could anyone fail to respond to their name?

"There's nothing to say. You're mine now."

"I know you're lonely."

Mallory watches carefully for his reaction. A "*what?*" look flashes across his face. Incredulous.

"What you're trying to do—it's lonely. You have a vision."

He seems distracted now, almost forgets about her breasts.

"You wanted to get beyond the rules. They were so suffocating."

"How do you know?"

Mallory feels a stab of triumph.

"I've seen you preach. You have a message that doesn't fit into any category."

"I've been in trouble all my life," he says.

"No wonder. You see beyond religion. Of course no one is going to understand."

For a second, he looks almost on the verge of tears. Then his face hardens.

"Bitch."

"Don't talk to me like that."

"You're a fucking bitch."

"Dolph—"

He slams out of the room, leaving her blouse open. And then it is dark again and there is no one. He has not brought her any food and she will not be able to hold her bladder for much longer. Already she smells herself, overripe, an odour of hair oil and glands.

She thinks of Mum and Dad. She doesn't want to, but she thinks of them.

Gradually the room gets light again.

SILVERNOR

He does not come back again for a long time.

Mallory has no choice but to piss herself. The shame nearly kills her.

Her mind turns.

Tell me who the Maiden met in the woods.

Well, child, come nearer and I'll tell you. On the fourteenth day of her fast, Maid Madeleine the Fair and Powerful received a clearer vision than ever before in a lifetime of startling prophecy. The Black King was about to dispatch a great force for evil, which would soon terrorize the people of Silvernor into cowering submission. The heinous wizard Dreadfall was the mastermind behind this great manifestation, which some say was conjured right out of the depths of his own dark and blighted mind.

"My liege!" the wizard cried. "'Tis a pleasure to look upon thy noble face again, O Anointed One!"

"Save your treacle, Dreadfall. The people are restive. They begin to doubt my authority." The Black King fingered his coarse, curling black beard with stubby fingers. "I will need an agent ... yes, an agent of my authority ..."

So where am I going with this? A dragon? Yeah, right, a dragon! It's crap, I know it's crap, but I have to hold on, I have to hold on to the story.

I just wish I had some paper. A pen.

Anything.

CHRIS

But Dolph doesn't come back with her next meal. The kid brings it in, walking with a bit of a swagger now, like a warden.

"Frank. Christ. Take me to the bathroom."

"You stink. What did you do, piss yourself?"

"I can't get to a toilet! What do you expect?"

"Shut up, bitch." He unties her wrists. She buttons up her blouse, her face smarting with shame that this kid should see her bra. Then he drags her to the bathroom as usual. Trying to push her bowel movement out takes forever, it's like a block of stone, and all the while the kid stands in the semi-open doorway and yells, "Come on, come on!"

She devours the white bread sandwich, peanut butter this time, no vegetables, no fruit, she'll get scurvy, but does that really matter when she's about to be murdered anyway?

"Frank, why are you doing this?"

"Don't call me that."

"I'll call you by your right name if you'll tell me." Mallory realizes in shock that her voice sounds just slightly seductive.

He looks at her in surprise.

"Chris."

Yes. She has won a point. A small one, but right now it's enough.

"Chris, why are you doing this? What's in it for you? Is he paying you?"

"He knows what he's doing. This is part of a plan."

"But that's crazy. This can't lead to anything good, unless there's a ransom or something. And my parents don't have any money. How can he be thinking straight?"

"You've seen him preach. And what he did for Annie. He has powers."

"What he did *to* Annie, you mean."

Rage flashes in his face and for a moment Mallory thinks he'll lash out at her again. She refuses to show any fear.

"Annie betrayed him. She had it coming."

"I think you've got that backwards."

"If you believe in someone, you stay loyal to them, no matter what."

Then Mallory remembers.

This is the queer kid. The one who confessed he was a homosexual. The scene comes flooding back into her mind. He went up to the front in that weird sleepwalking way and fell on his knees, blubbering in a pleading voice, oh, God, take this away from me, make me normal like everyone else, I don't want to be queer any more! The Rev laid his hands on him and concentrated so hard, smoke seemed to waft from the top of his head.

"Be healed," he said.

So now poor Chris must believe he isn't queer any more, that he's cured. That the Rev purged him of all his deviant desires.

"Chris."

"Yeah."

"You ever get lonely?"

"None of your fucking business."

"I mean—do the other kids make fun of you and stuff?"

"What's it to you?"

"It's just that—I think I know what it feels like. The kids had a name for me. They used to call me *manwoman*. I guess they thought I looked like a guy."

"Well, you do."

"They ever call you stuff?"

"Like you care."

"But I know what it feels like."

Chris sits down next to her on the army cot. This is completely unexpected. Mallory's gut clenches.

"I get called a fag all the time. Like it's the worst thing in the world you can be. Like you're not a real person or something."

149

"That must be terrible."

"I want to fucking die sometimes."

"Ever cut yourself?"

He looks shocked.

"How did you know?"

Mallory unbuttons the cuffs of her blouse and pulls up her sleeves. The sight of her arms is startling. It's a battlefield of scars, long thin razor-tracings, jagged scissor-marks like raised bolts of lightning, round healed burns.

"Holy shit."

"You ever do that?"

"Not like that. You're one fucked-up bitch." But there is admiration in his voice.

"Chris. Do you have to tie me up again? I can't get out of here. There's no way out. The ropes hurt like hell and I'm going nuts from the boredom. Can't you leave me untied for just a little while? You can put them back on before the Rev comes back."

He looks at her steadily.

Then he gets up and leaves. Just leaves. She is free. Or as free as one can be while locked in a stifling little cell. She can stand up, sit down at will. The feeling is so exhilarating she bursts into sobs for the first time since all this happened.

She is giddy with her new freedom, happier than she has been in years.

WINDOW

The first thing she does is check the tiny window. It's high up, difficult for her to reach even on her toes, and reinforced with a fine metal mesh. Smashing through it would be nearly impossible, and she could never fit through to escape. But could she scream? Sound carries. Could she throw something outside?

She begins to sort methodically through all the old junk piled in the room. There must be something here that will help her, or at least give her an idea what to do next.

Then darkness seeps into the room again, and the helpless feeling crowds back into her head. The blackness increases moment by moment. Her sense of power drains away.

If the Rev finds her like this, walking around and planning her escape, he'll kill her. But she can't tie up her own hands.

I'm going to be killed.

Shut up. We have to think of something.

Fear is her enemy. It will eat her alive. She must calm her gut, tame her mind, hold on.

DRAGON

Tell me about the Dragon.

The evil wizard Dreadfall conjured a great scourge on the village—a force so overwhelming that it left the good people impotent and cowering. In this state of raw terror, even the most valiant of them were soft in the hands of the Pretender.

Hellbane the Hideous was his name, and nine heads had he, which reared in heinous ugliness. Each head bespoke an aspect of human evil: pride, avarice, lust, sloth, gluttony, anger and envy; false worship, which distorts the primal love of God; and by far the worst and ugliest of all, the Ninth Head, which represented sins against children.

Now I have told you how precious and well-loved were the children of Silvernor. But something began to curdle when this ugly Head reared above the community. The people lost touch with the sacred value of their young, and began to neglect and abuse them. The children of Silvernor became the playthings of the Black King, who took pleasure in acts of unspeakable inhumanity and perversion.

Even Maid Madeleine with all her visionary powers fell under this chill shadow. One afternoon the Pretender hammered at her door, interrupting her preparation of herbs and physics. Though she rushed to lock it, she was not quite fast enough, and the hulking figure burst through, his chill shadow dropping over the Maiden's head like a dark and suffocating veil.

SAY MY NAME

Chris is softening. At least a bit. He hasn't tied her up again and sometimes they talk a little before he shuffles out of the room and leaves her alone again.

The day he brings her a blank Hilroy scribbler and a pen, she wants to fall down and weep at his feet with gratitude.

The first thing she does is write down the last two chapters of *Silvernor*, flawed or not. She holds back, or tries to, knowing she can fill this book in a single day. So she writes small and close, and rations herself. A paragraph, and stop; a paragraph, and stop.

She aches to keep a journal, but knows she can't afford the paper.

Still, it is salvation to be able to write. She can almost forget the stink of the place, mould and pee and pipes, and the fact that she is sometimes forced to use a plastic garbage pail as a toilet.

But hope is a bad habit in this place. Chris comes in, grim, with no food. He starts tying her hands again, in spite of her protests.

"Hey, Chris—let's talk about this."

"Shut up."

When he puts the blindfold back on, his hands graze her face, almost caressing her. She feels a slick of fear on her skin, panic rising in her throat like a living creature trying to push its way up and out.

Then a hundred more years of waiting. Mallory talks to herself, out loud this time, to keep her grip.

"I'll get out of this. He's not going to get me. God, help me out of this. If you're there, please listen for the first time in my bloody life. I need you. I need you to help me. Help me out of here. Send someone. Make the Rev crack. Make Chris talk.

Anything. Just get me out. Glory be to God, amen. Come on, you fuck, *help* me."

When the door cracks open, she smells smoke and gin and knows who it is.

"Don't hurt me," she says. The words fly out of her mouth before she can check them. He sits down on the cot. Silent. She wishes he would say something, anything. Even abuse is better than this. Then she feels his hand on her belly and flinches.

He grabs the collar of her blouse and rips. Buttons fly. Mallory gasps. A button hits her on the chin. Then he heaves himself on top of her.

She can hear the belt unbuckling, a minute clink of silver metal. Then a zip.

He begins to tug her pants down. Mallory smells a high skunky stink like cat spray and realizes it's his male scent, oily and glandular. She thinks, if this is sex, no one could like it. I will die.

I will die.

"Say my name," she says.

A grunt of response.

"Say my name. Say it."

He has pulled back.

"I want you to say my name."

The idea is completely insane, it will never work, she will die in an instant, as soon as he can wrap his hands around her throat.

"Mallory."

"Say it again."

"Mallory." He says it softly. Almost reverently.

He withdraws. Mallory wonders if he has lost his erection.

"Dolph, you really don't want to hurt me."

A long, shuddering intake of breath.

"Why don't you let me go? You know this is wrong."

Is he picturing it? Giving himself up? He hasn't seriously harmed her yet. Has he?

Is it time for him to give up the dream? Stop running? Let down at last, let the nightmare end?

He grabs her hair and gives it a savage yank backwards. "Don't play with me."

"Dolph ..."

"Stop saying that."

"But it's your name."

"You're mine now."

"I'm a human being. I belong to God."

This stops him.

Maybe she has hit on something.

"I'm God's child, Dolph."

"Shut up about it."

"What made you want to be a minister?"

"What?"

"What made you decide to be a minister in the first place? You must have felt a calling. What was that like?"

He has nothing to say. Nothing.

"God will forgive you," says Mallory.

He escapes from the room, slamming the door.

Mallory is left tied. But still alive. Still breathing.

THE SWORD

Once more, she must write in her head.

Tell me about the Sword.

Long did Madeleine the Fair and Powerful kneel in devoted prayer in the depths of the wilderness. The horror had been shown to her: a mighty Dragon with nine evil heads, which she must find a way to destroy so that the good people of Silvernor could be released from the hideous spell that held them frozen in horror.

At the end of forty days of prayer and contemplation, the Maiden began to walk.

Her heart told her the way. She walked for seven days, down a long, dark and tortuous path, which took her deep into the earth.

At the end of a labyrinthine twist of tunnel that was as convoluted as a bowel, the Maiden's footsteps halted at a place that glowed curiously in the darkness.

She saw a huge stone, its obsidian bulk crowned by the gleaming hilt of an ancient, ornately carved silver sword.

HERO

By the time Chris returns, her wrists are raw from struggling, her neck still stabbing her at the slightest motion. A raw chunk of hair and scalp lies on the cot beside her.

When he unties her, she has to restrain herself from throwing her arms around him.

He brings her food. He releases her. He lets her see again. He is her hero. She almost loves him. This sullen, pimply, guilty kid who hates being a fag.

"So when did you figure out that you were queer?"

"I'm not. It's gone now."

"Bullshit. You want to believe that, but it isn't true."

"What do you know about it?"

"I almost had sex with a girl."

He looks interested. "So? You going to tell me about it?"

"First you tell me what it's like with a guy."

"I've never done it. I mean, not with a guy."

"Not with anybody, you mean."

The scene is completely bizarre: two people in a room, one held captive with half the buttons of her blouse ripped off, and they're bantering almost like lovers.

"I haven't found anybody I like yet."

"You ever made out with a girl?"

He looks shocked. "What are you saying?"

"Nothing. Just thought you might like to try it."

"You want something."

"What?"

"You're just trying to get something out of me."

"What do you mean? Come over here."

He sits next to her on the cot, looking at her as if she's a poisonous reptile, yet fascinated.

She takes his hand and puts it on her small right breast.

Nothing happens.

He pulls his hand away.

"I guess you really are queer, then."

"Shut up. I just don't like feeling up strangers."

"We aren't strangers. I'm getting to know you pretty well, Chris. I don't think too many people understand you."

"Crap."

"The Rev's not in the house all the time, is he?"

"Like I'd tell you."

"Why don't you let me go upstairs? I'll come back down right away. I'm going crazy in this place. And I really need a bath."

He looks like he's considering it. Mallory can never quite believe what words can do, simple words, if you only dare to use them.

He leads her upstairs, keeping a tight grip on her arm. It is ecstasy to walk up the stairs, to hear birds outside, to see sunlight streaming through clear windows.

He lets her use the shower. She feels unbelievable pleasure in soaping her entire body, washing her gritty hair and rinsing it, drying herself with the fat plush towel. Though her stomach looks caved-in, her legs scrawny as sticks. How long has she been a captive, living on scraps of bad food, tied up like a dog? Weeks?

She hates putting the same stale clothes back on. But feels more human now, her skin no longer crawling.

When she comes out of the bathroom, she stops short. Chris isn't there. She can hear him rattling around in the kitchen.

Mallory can't believe his carelessness. He slipped up, he didn't watch.

She lunges for the front door, pulls it open. Out, she's *out!* She hurls herself down the sidewalk, running faster than she knew she could. When she reaches the street, her legs go out from under her and she hits cement, hard.

Chris drags her bodily back into the house. She screams and screams.

Just as the door shuts behind them, she catches a glimpse of an old lady coming out onto her porch.

Someone knows.

She'll get out of here.

She will.

She *will*.

NOTHING

Then, nothing.

Tied up again, blindfolded, but this time he even puts the gag back in her mouth to shut up her screaming. Then he walks out.

Stupid! Stupid, stupid, stupid. She could have used the phone in the hall, called someone before Chris noticed. She could have screamed out the door, Help me! Bolting was so panicky, so wrong. Now whatever trust she has carefully built up with him is blown. Who knows when he will be back?

Mr. and Mrs. Mardling arrive home from their trip to Toronto to find the house an unspeakable, chaotic mess. Victor is virtually incoherent, off his medication, filthy. Nola is nowhere around. Mallory has disappeared.

Mrs. Mardling takes two pills and a shot of sherry and lies down in the bedroom. Sam Mardling picks up the phone and calls the police.

HELLBANE

The troubles at Silvernor were not the sort to last for a few months, or even a year. The reign of terror waged by the Pretender and his terrible companion, the black wizard Dreadfall, went on for year upon year, until the good people of the town were hard-pressed to remember what it felt like to be alive in times of freedom and joy.

Trust became a thing of the past. Silence overtook merriment and laughter. Even the posture of the people changed, with young lads and lasses plodding about like old folk, and old folk ceasing to walk at all. Children stopped looking like children, and took on a hollow-eyed, skin-stretched look, as if they were underfed and underloved. No child was ever sure whose house the Pretender would descend upon next. No one spoke of the fact, but everyone knew that he treated tender children like mere wenches, forcing them into behaviour they could not possibly comprehend.

The darkness deepened, and every time any citizens of Silvernor showed a spark of spirit, Hellbane would rear up in all his terrible glory and frighten them back into meek submission again. It was a curious thing, but after the Dragon was gone, disappearing in a grey trail of foul and greasy smoke, no one was sure just what they had seen. It was as if the wizard Dreadfall had the power to make all the people dream the same dream, while their eyes were open and they were quite awake.

Even Maid Madeleine with all her powers of vision began to doubt her own eyes, and wondered to herself, is the Dragon real? She had taken to giving the Pretender all her most precious herbal remedies and physics as a sort of ransom for the children of Silvernor. A bag of bounty might hold off his vile actions for a day, or a week. Then his lust would flame anew—a lust greater even than his lust for wealth and power. The children could not speak of their pain, for it was a Secret—a deep, malignant secret with no reason, no compassion, and no end.

THE BOTTOM

Silence.

Darkness.

A roaring, a rhythmical whooshing, internal, eternal. The singing of her own heart.

It croons in her ears, intimate, insistent.

She wishes the roar would stop.

Just *stop*.

DOLPH

Then the door cracks.

Now she will die.

Try to die bravely, without screaming and thrashing.

But nothing happens, except breathing. Wheezy, shivery breaths. They go on endlessly.

Then he begins to free her.

When she can see him again, she notices the white in his hair, his sunken face, and realizes something.

Things are not as they seem. Not at all.

In fact, she has had it backwards all the time.

She is holding him.

She is holding *him*.

With her in here, he can't live. His life revolves around her.

"Dolph," she says.

He looks down at the floor.

"Dolph, do you want to pray?"

He grabs his gut, something flying up his throat, some awful godly force, something left in him that writhes and tortures.

"Let's pray together. Dear God. Only You can understand why we find ourselves in this place today."

Dolph begins to sob. The sound is scary, raw as a sawtooth wheel carving through the muscles of his control.

"Only You know the end of the story. But we believe Your mercy is here with us today. We believe in Your love. We believe in Your forgiveness. We know that Your goodness will prevail even in this place."

A gasp, a barking sob wrenched up, uncontainable.

Mallory's chest feels like it will burst.

"God, we know You will forgive everything that has happened

164

here. Your ways are unsearchable. Your mercy knows no bounds. Touch us with Your grace."

She reaches out, and puts her hand on the top of Dolph's head.

He seems to shrink. Then explodes, flinging her hand away. His fist smashes into her face, knocking her into the wall.

Then an ungodly cry from the depths of his being: "Christ! Christ! Christ!"

He rakes at his own flesh, his face flushing and contorting into the dark face of a primate.

"Christ! Christ! Christ!"

He throws himself on the concrete floor and smashes his head down. And down. And down.

"*Christ!*"

She knows it is his prayer.

THE RELEASE

It is easier to sleep with a concussion. Or at least that is what she thinks this is, this blissful, unstrung feeling, this drifting.

She has slipped the leash of Time.

She breaks the surface and the room heaves, a blur. She feels sick, but there is nothing inside her to throw up. She is aware of a vague shape on the floor like a blight, with a dark pool around it. A singing sound in her ears, a sustained keening.

Then she slips down, under the heavy press of the water again. She is a whale in the deeps, silently cruising, huge and beautiful.

Then, a blast of light.

"Holy Jesus," a voice says.

THE LIGHT

It will take her a long time to realize what happened.

In the place of injury, of deep damage, she drifts to and fro, visiting Life, then Death, as possibilities.

Both look intriguing. She has no awareness that all this is caused by bleeding in her brain, that hospital monitors hum all around her, that her own father fell on his knees beside her bed, sobbing that his little girl is alive, alive, and that nothing else matters at all.

The old lady on the porch is her unlikely saviour. Her suspicions about what had been going on in that house were confirmed when the police forced the door. Chris broke down and bawled like an infant, confessing everything.

The Rev lies in a prison infirmary, closer to death than Mallory. His skull has been fractured. He slammed his head with terrific force, as if trying to smash out the badness, or kill the intolerable good that writhed within him.

Mallory drifts towards Life. It is a mixed place, glinting with light and dark, beauty and bliss intermingled with manifold shocks, malign surprises. It baffles her, but she feels drawn to it, and sits in awe.

She moves towards Death. It looks to her like a hall of mirrors, full of reflections and reflections, as if it is not the end of anything, but a deeper complexity even than the enigma of Life. She knows she will go there, enter in when It decides, be swallowed, and come out the other side, strangely, to another beginning.

There is no sense of being able to choose. Both forces own her. They are in her and she is of them, equally. She drifts.

Mallory is being prayed for. Can she feel it? It is a sensation gentle as a rose softly expanding in her chest.

Energy whizzes and crackles in the air. People come in one by one and stand beside her bed. Mum. Dad. Gail. Cal. Kathy. Even Simon, who whispers his prayers out loud.

He has never prayed before, so is not sure how to do this. But tries to anyway.

She hesitates, between poles, uncertain.

She moves towards Life.

Her eyes open.

PART III:
DR. RUBENS

FAMOUS

And then, for just a little while, Mallory is famous.

As soon as she can sit up and talk, the kids start pouring in. Not just the kids from the Club. Real kids. Average kids. Kids who fit in, who belong.

The same kids, some of them, who called her "manwoman" and "fuckface" and "cunt."

How can she tell them to get out of her room? This is the first time she has ever been acceptable, let alone popular.

She hates her own weakness, but lets them stay. She lets them stay even though she knows they have been brought here by a combination of pity, horror and fascination, and not because they like her at all. She won't say whether or not the Rev sexually assaulted her. Holding it back is much more powerful than telling. But she implies damage. Terrible damage.

She wants to sustain her fame for as long as she can.

When a young woman from the local press interviews her, she is on a high like she has never known in her life. She hears herself talking about things that didn't happen: "They starved me." "I went days without seeing anyone." "He kept saying he was going to kill me." Well, it might be true: she did lose her sense of time. The food was scarce, and bad. And wasn't she afraid every minute that the Rev would lose his grip and murder her?

"And you managed to keep your sanity by . . . writing a story?"

"It's a novel. *The Secret of Silvernor, or Maid Madeleine's Honour.* It's a fantasy for adults, kind of like *The Lord of the Rings.*"

"A novel! That's impressive."

"Yes, it's my first."

"May I say that you are an extraordinary young woman."

But none of that gets into the article, which sticks to bald facts.

There is no mention of the novel. Probably they thought it would be too weird. Mallory is horribly let down. She feels cheated.

As soon as the Rev is found out, people begin to come forward. All kinds of people. Mallory thinks they were too chickenshit, or too blinded by the shiny veneer of his authority, to say anything before.

I suspected he was up to something crooked from the very start.

Didn't I try to tell people he was a bad apple?

He's a psychopath. We always knew it.

What happened to Mallory is monstrous, and she feels monstrous, but the picture of the Rev in the *Kennewick Standard* makes him look like Frankenstein, with a big seam across his forehead and a crystalline vacancy in the eyes.

Apparently, he has lost the power of speech. His words have dried up. Stopped in his throat, perhaps forever.

Or is he faking? It would be hard to fake the slack lips, the stoned eyes and passive posture of the deeply brain-damaged.

This means he will never go to trial. He has escaped, at the cost of his wholeness.

By the time Mallory can go home again to her tearful mum and jittery, blustering dad, three things have happened.

One: more than half the summer is over. How did it get to be August? It is one more mean trick, a trick of Time itself.

Two: the Rev has been committed to the Kennewick Regional Sanitorium. Unable to look after himself, any kin long since vanished from weariness or fear, he is alone in the world. Mallory feels a mixture of repugnance, relief and stupid, irrational guilt.

Three: Victor has gone to the same place, but a different wing, for intractable schizophrenia. He is on a drug cocktail now that makes him do the mental-patient shuffle, spine curved like Gramma's, always looking down at his feet.

Mallory begs Mum and Dad not to make her go there. They

relent; she might see the Reverend Fletcher, after all, being taken out on a leash for an airing or something.

But this means Mallory never sees Victor. In a sense, he has died, just like Annie.

But no one knows whether Annie is actually dead. There is no evidence, no body, in spite of an intensive investigation. The house where Mallory was imprisoned is ripped apart, the backyard excavated. All the kids at the Club have to answer a multitude of uncomfortable questions. But no one has much to say.

Chris Cooper, her jailer, is being held at a juvenile detention centre. At times Mallory yearns to see him, then feels bewildered at this urge. She hates him. She wishes him dead. Then he tries to hang himself, and Mallory wonders how powerful a death wish can be.

But he survives, cut down in time. He can't talk for several weeks, his voice a mere rasp.

Mallory knows how she is supposed to feel. According to her classmates, her teachers, even the local newspaper, she is the heroine, the victorious figure. She is free now, free to live the rest of her life without a trace of terror, anxiety or dread. She has won.

THE HOLE

But there's nowhere to go. The Club has scattered. Everyone has disappeared into an invisible hole in the fabric of the everyday. Simon has left town—has he gone to Toronto? Cal went to stay with his grandmother in Calgary. *Calgary!* What a lame place to go.

Mallory is alone, as alone as the Rev, or Victor, or poor damaged Chris in his hell of guilt and confusion.

I can't fucking sleep.

I can't fucking *sleep*, and it's like three in the goddamn morning and my head is pounding, and I know even if I *did* get off to sleep, which would be a freaking miracle, I'd have the same nightmare I've been having every night for the past two weeks.

I'm tied to that goddamn army cot, my wrists bound to the iron frame, and it's dark and I'm alone, but I have this huge belly and I'm in agonizing pain and I realize I'm about to have a baby.

A baby. A goddamn *baby*, and I don't even remember having sex.

I push and heave and cry out, and there's this big hand pushing down on my stomach but I don't know who is attached to the hand. Then finally this big dark head forces its way out between my legs, and as it comes out it sort of twists around, and I can see these two glowing fiendish eyes straight out of some late-night horror movie like *Rosemary's Baby*.

I scream and scream and push and push and the rest of the body slowly slithers out, and it's all fat and slick and covered with long blackish hair. What's the word? *Simian*. It looks like a baby ape. Then all of a sudden Annie is standing beside the bed and tending to the baby. Wearing a butcher's white apron daubed with blood. She severs the umbilical cord with a big pair of scissors, holds the baby up by the feet and slaps its bottom.

Only the sound it's making isn't a baby sound at all, but this godawful unearthly mannish howl, like someone whose vocal cords have been French fried. I know that voice, I know who it belongs to. Annie looks pleased. She smiles at me and says, "It's a boy."

When she holds the baby up to my face for me to see, it has a huge head with a seam running across it, and crystalline eyes, like the eyes of a wolf caught in the headlights.

I wake up screaming, and at first Mum comes running in, saying, "Mallory! Mallory! Stop that! The neighbours will hear you. You must calm down!" But after a few nights in a row of the same thing, she lets me scream. One night Dad yells "*Shut up*" in the general direction of my room.

So things are getting back to normal, more or less. But with a difference.

The difference is, everything freaks me. Shadows freak me. When I am brushing my teeth, I feel like someone is coming up behind me. When I lie in bed, my shoulder frozen to my chin, I feel as if someone will burst through the door at any second.

I can hear my pulse in my ears. *Woosh-ah, woosh-ah, woosh-ah*, all night long. Until I feel so crazy I have to get up.

I'm tired as shit all day, and bored and scared at the same time, a combination I never knew was humanly possible until now. It's summer and everyone has scattered, and no one is talking about the Rev because they think that would be bad for me, it will only upset me to be reminded. I overhear Mum and Dad buzzing away at each other all the time, but they stop the minute I come in the room—"*sh-sh*, here she comes."

One of the worst things about the entire experience is that the police took my notebook with the chapters from *Silvernor* in it, and I can't recreate them from memory. I seem to be stuck or frozen or something. The words just won't come out. I'm thinking of burning the whole thing anyway. But what else is there to do? I can't watch TV all the time, stupid kids' shows like *Cap'n Jolly* and *Jingles* and *Milky the Clown* and reruns of lame sitcoms like *I Married Joan* and *December Bride.* And panel shows. Panel shows are the worst. Will the real Adolph Hitler please stand up?

I try to go for walks or even go swimming, but I just get too freaked. I don't want to be naked—it frightens me. Even taking a shower is hard, so I have to go fast, scrub my skin like I'm washing down a dirty wall or something. When I go to the dentist's for my annual checkup, he says to me, "Mallory, have you been clenching?"

"Clenching?"

"Grinding your jaw. You know, in the night."

"Why would I do that?"

"Oh, it happens for no particular reason. We find it runs in families."

"Why, no, doctor, I'm not aware that I'm clenching or grinding."

"You have a hairline fracture in your molar here. And here's another one. We might have to fit you for a night guard."

Great. Another gag. It'll give me something to chew on. Something to muffle my screams? Now there's a thought. Mum will appreciate that.

Weird things go through my head. I have other dreams about Annie, that I see her in a crowd, but when I try to follow her she disappears.

One time I dreamed I saw her crying. She was looking down at a dark splotch on the floor. I had this crazy thought that she'd miscarried the baby.

And the Rev. I don't want to think about the Rev, a drooling zombie in a mental institution, but I do think about him, all the time, and I can't help but feel like it was me who put him there.

I did it, I turned his rage around, bent it, deflected it away from me and back to himself. And it could have killed him, but God let him live. (Or was it the other guy? The so-called Devil. Sometimes I can't tell the two of them apart, they look so much alike.)

And Chris. I guess I did something to him, too. Fucked with his head or something. I feel sorry for him, but sort of repulsed, too. He's so pathetic, he just caved in instantly and told them everything, no loyalty at all. I can't respect that.

I don't hate the Rev. I guess I should, but what I feel mostly is bafflement. I don't know how a person whose life revolves around God could go so sour, so poisonous. Maybe he went insane from too much God? Flew too close to the sun? What is it about God that makes people so crazy? Is there just too great a contrast between divine perfection and their own fucked-up, wormy state? Do they think they have to be like that themselves, all-loving, all-forgiving? Some kind of freaking saint?

I prayed a lot when I was in the room. But in the room, I did a lot of other things too: peed myself, ate bread with blue mould on it, wrote brilliant chapters in my head that slipped and tilted when I tried to put them down on the page. When you're desperate, you do desperate things. You're pushed to extremes.

Now I don't even know who or what there is to pray to. There's no Big Guy in the Sky. That much I know. Maybe God is just the great Whatever. The "is" of things, or the life force or something, but the only trouble with that is, the life force doesn't give a rat's ass about individuals. Look at what happens in nature. Creatures devour each other, rip each other's tendons apart just to keep the whole intricate interlocking cycle going. The weak don't last a day, and you'd better not show any vulnerability at all, or you too will be eliminated. It's survival of the heartless. Then what? What is there? All this is there, the reality of everything, and I can't believe there's just nothing behind it at all.

I'd be a humanist, but humans are too fucked to believe in. Too full of holes. We didn't create this mess. No, this particular mess named humanity must have been created by a power far greater than ourselves.

Or infinitely more cruel.

INGA RUBENS

It's Dewla, the usually mild and gutless Dewla, who finally puts her foot down.

"I have had *enough* of this!" She slams down her teacup so that the Red Rose inside it sloshes over the sides and slops onto the tablecloth.

Mallory freezes.

"You're always crying. Always going around with this long, hangdog face. For God's sake, girl, you need to buck up. Everything turned out all right."

Mallory crumples.

"You're a young girl with your whole life ahead of you. You're smart, you've got a brain, you're even starting to develop a figure. You've got to stop all this moping around and get on with things."

"Mum ..."

"Mallory." This is one of the rare times Mum touches her. And it feels like electric shock on her body when she brushes back a lock of her lank dark hair. The longing this stirs up in her is nearly intolerable. *Mum.* "I'm going to phone this Dr. Rubens. I know you like to make fun of her, but I really think you need to talk to somebody. Who knows, she might be able to help you feel better."

"She'll give me pills."

"Well, what's wrong with that? The right medicine might help you get your spirits back."

Spirits. Mallory sees the spectre of Annie hovering over her bed and wonders if she should take all the Librium Dr. Rubens prescribed before this happened.

With her luck, probably there wouldn't be enough to finish the job.

She doesn't want to see her again. The bloodless lips, the cold eyes, the accent thick as some cabbage-choked Slavic soup phlegming up her consonants so that a simple "r" becomes a drawn-out gargle.

But there is no one. No one else who knows anything about this. She is dying.

When she walks into the office, everything looks different, bizarrely different, even though her intellect tells her nothing has changed: there is the familiar pale reproduction of a van Gogh painting of irises on the wall, the same ugly gooseneck lamp and stolid old bookcase in the corner. When she sits down, the black leather chair studded with brass nails emits the same pathetic little squeak.

"Mallory." The inflection rises at the end, almost like a question, but muted, almost respectful.

Mallory stares at her. Dr. Rubens is used to her, enough that she knows Mallory's blank refusal to respond is an attempt to cope with what must feel like yet another violation.

"How do you feel today?"

Mallory's eyes wander around the room, then alight on a spot between Dr. Rubens's eyebrows.

"Like crap."

"That's honest."

"Would I lie to you?"

"Mallory. Vee know you've been through a lot since the last time you came here. Perhaps vee need to talk about it."

"Do you really want to hear?"

The smell of the place, flooding her pants with pee, praying that the ordeal be over, even if she died, devouring dry bologna and bad bread, aching to hear Chris's footsteps outside the door of the airless little tomb.

"I really vant to hear."

"I miss Chris." She drops the bombshell first. Let Rubens think she's mentally deranged for not wanting to mention rope burn, hunger, isolation and the constant unrelenting terror of being raped or killed.

"Chris vas the young man who brought you food every day."

"He was my jailer. He didn't come every day, either, I could tell, even though after a while I lost track of time. He was this wimpy little kid just following orders like some bloody Nazi, and queer into the bargain."

"And you miss him."

"Christ." Mallory does not want to cry, but something has seized her, something huge. She sits inside a big hand, and if she dares to move, she knows it will crush her to death. So she stays absolutely still.

"Vhat do you miss about him?"

"The . . . sense of hope." The key turning in the door would flood her with a radiant, insane joy, joy unnatural and unreal. "I'd see him in the doorway and then I'd smell food, and I'd want to put my arms around him or something, even though I hated the little shit."

"He vas keeping you alive."

"Yeah. After a fashion. Tied up and in terror."

"Did you talk?"

"Yeah, we did. It was weird. After a while it was almost like we were friends and in the whole mess together or something. Even though that was total bullshit, because I found out later the Rev was paying him all the time. I wanted to know his name, I wanted to know some stuff about him."

"And did he tell you?"

"I was freaking amazed at how much he told me. He started to become a real person after a while, not just this jailer who had power over me."

"That meant you had power over him."

"What?"

"You insisted he be a real person, a human being, not just zome animal keeper. And that means he had to see you as human, too."

"I just . . . needed somebody to talk to."

"You vere saving yourself."

"But he got *caught!*" Mallory's body jackknifes with the

intensity of wrenched-back emotion catapulting to the surface. "I tricked him into letting me go upstairs. He let his guard down. I got out of there for long enough that the game was up, he was found out."

"Which was only right."

"*No!*" The spasms are too powerful for her to manage. For a moment she can't speak. "He got caught. They put him in jail and he tried to hang himself." As she speaks her voice climbs steadily higher and higher until it is the voice of a small child. "Fucking hang himself! His life is ruined and it's all my fault."

"Mallory. I vant you to listen to me now. Vhat I am about to say is very important."

After a huge, shuddering intake of breath, Mallory listens.

"Vhat you did, you had to do. You had to befriend him in order to survive. You vere in this tiny little room together. A prison cell. He vas your only chance. Your only hope."

"I hate him."

"Yes, you hate him, and you love him too, because he gave you food, he kept you alive, he even talked to you and began to treat you like you vere a person. But zat was *you*, Mallory. You saved yourself. Zat took courage. Enormous courage."

Rubens's eyes are brimming, her voice thick with emotion. Mallory realizes she is struggling not to weep.

"I'm sorry," the doctor says.

"Don't be sorry."

"Vhat you did—it vas remarkable."

"But I feel so bad about it. And the Rev—I feel like I did that, too."

"He did it to himself."

"But I made him do it."

"Vhat vere you supposed to do? Let him kill you?"

"He's an idiot now, in a mental hospital. Forever, probably."

"It vas his choice."

"Does that mean there was good in him? Or what?"

"Who knows." Dr. Rubens takes her glasses off and rubs her

eyes. "I don't know everyzing, Mallory, I just try to help people. In ze end, maybe he couldn't do ze vorst. Is zat goodness?"

"I'm not sure I know what goodness is."

"But you prayed."

"How did you know that?"

"Call it a hunch."

"I didn't even know who or what I was praying to. I still don't know. If there's a God, I don't know how He or She or It can allow things to get so fucked up. But I did pray, really hard, all the time, when I wasn't writing the novel in my head."

"You kept hoping."

"I'm not sure it was hope. Maybe just some animal thing, a reflex? But it was more than that."

"You vere holding on to life."

"But life is a crappy deal."

"Not necessarily." Dr. Rubens looks straight into her eyes. The effect is startling. "Life can surprise you. Vee can never see ze end of ze story. And things change. Zey change in amazing vays. You say life is a crappy deal. But Mallory, zo much of it is zo good. It's good beyond anysing you can even imagine."

Mallory aches to believe it.

"Mallory, you vill make a life for yourself. And it vill be extraordinary. If you can survive zis, you can survive anysing. You vill use zat mind of yours, and people vill hear you. I guarantee it."

"But how can you be so sure? Why are you saying all this?"

Something changes in Dr. Rubens's face. Everything softens, the hard lines around her mouth vanish and her eyes cloud. "During ze var, ven I vas a girl in Holland—

Mallory is stunned.

The war.

"Vee vere very fortunate, vee escaped ze camps, and zo many people vere not zo lucky. But it was hard, Mallory. Very hard. I heard stories. I heard about a vhoman, she lost her baby, and she knew she would starve to death very soon. So she . . . Mallory, I can't say zis. She did vhat she had to do."

Mallory swallows. Shock hits her like a literal blow.

"Vass zat a crime? I don't think zo. Not under the circumstances."

Mallory's mouth opens and closes, but no sound will come out.

"Vee vere so lucky, vee knew a baker. Zo every morning, vee gave away haff our bread to zomeone. A different neighbour each day. It was such a small thing."

"No. No, it wasn't a small thing." Mallory can't stop the tears that are now freely pouring down her face.

"But the point is, Mallory, vee do vhat vee haf to do to survive. You used your mind to set yourself free. Freedom, Mallory—zat is a precious thing. It is life itself."

They sit quietly for some time. Neither of them needs to speak. It is as if a massive swell has washed over them, but they are still standing. Mallory feels an awe, like looking at stars. The feeling is strange and shivery and she doesn't fully understand it, but wants it to stay.

At the end of the session, Dr. Rubens bends and gravely, formally, kisses her on the cheek. Mallory looks up at her and feels something unquenchable blazing inside her chest. With a thrill of shock, she recognizes the feeling as a kind of love.

When she goes home that afternoon, she finds she is able to write again, and picks up the thread of the *Silvernor* story from where she left off before the whole ordeal began.

SEPTEMBER

The first day of class, and a strange sense of reunion.

But no Annie. An ache, like the raw empty socket of a pulled tooth.

There will never be an Annie. Mallory feels it. She dreams of the corpse, hidden in an upstairs hall closet. Dreams of dragging it out into the hallway, where Mum discovers it and screams with horror.

But her mother is nearly oblivious, as she has always been. Mallory wonders if Mum does not know how to love, or at least how to show it. The chasm between them is immense, but Mallory cannot bridge it any more than Mum can.

She sees Gail. She sees Kathy. Both look different, sound different. They're sort of weird with each other. Awkward. "Oh . . . hullo." It's a funny vibe. What is the etiquette for addressing someone after a murder? There is no road map for what they can say to each other.

Yet Mallory feels she is being whispered about.

Then: shock of shocks. *Simon.* To find him here fills her with a tempestuous joy, and she wants to embrace him like a comrade in arms, but she doesn't.

"Mallie. Hey."

"Simon. I was wondering if I'd ever see you again."

"We're in the same class."

"*What?*"

"I'm back in grade twelve. Kind of where I got off."

"Why in the world are you back in school?" Simon is immensely old, Mallory thinks, nearly eighteen.

"Fuck, I don't know. The summer sucked. I hitchhiked around. Tried to sell some of my artwork on the street in Toronto. Got beat up a couple of times. This old guy hit on me, tried to . . . you know."

"That sounds . . ."

"Hey, it was nothing compared to what happened to you."

Mallory's eyes flood with tears. It hits her so unexpectedly, the grief, the shock. Then she is all right again.

"I survived. And so did you."

"I figure it can't kill me to get some sort of a formal education. I was just fucking lost before. And that's not good enough. Besides—you're here. That'll be a saving grace."

Mallory has never thought of herself as a saving grace before.

"How's the book coming?"

"Coming. I've done another seven chapters."

"Right on."

"I'm going to need more illustrations."

He grins. "I'll try to fit it into my busy schedule." Then he embraces her, scooping her up in his arms and lifting her off her feet. He kisses her cheek with such spontaneous affection that she gasps.

Walking to class, someone stops her short in the locker-lined hallway.

"Mallory."

It's Karen. Karen Anfield, the golden princess of grade eleven, the cheerleader, the one with the straight white teeth and brilliant blonde hair, the one who would never give her the time of day.

"Yes?" She braces for an inquisition. Or maybe another onslaught.

"I heard about what happened to you in the summer."

"Oh. I . . ."

"I just wanted to tell you . . ."

There is a kind of aura around the two of them, a strange, sudden, nearly impossible intimacy. Karen talking to Mallory: it goes against the laws of the universe. All the other kids stop digging around in their lockers to notice.

"At first I felt sorry for you, you know? 'Oh, Mallory Mardling, I kind of knew she'd end up in some sort of trouble. Hanging out with all those losers.'"

Rage flashes up in Mallory's chest. Fuck Karen Anfield, fuck her to death. She doesn't need Karen; she doesn't need anyone. She is in this completely alone.

"Then I heard about what happened, how you were kidnapped and got out of that place. I read about it in the paper."

Kidnapped? Mallory has never used that term, in her own mind. But isn't that exactly what happened?

"I just want to tell you . . . look, I really admire what you did, I admire your courage. That took guts, to stand up to those guys like that."

Mallory has no idea what to say. She notices Karen eyeing the other kids furtively. It looks bad, her talking to Mallory, but she just has to say this, she has to. She lowers her voice carefully so no one can overhear.

"I just think you're . . . I think I was wrong about you. I used to think you were a complete loser. I mean . . . Mallory Mardling! The other kids . . . you have no idea! I don't know how to say this, I'm sorry . . ." Karen is blushing, her face darkened by more than embarrassment.

Mallory can see how much this is costing her. She has an impulse to make it easier for her. "S'okay. You don't have to tell me this."

"I never could've done that, what you did. I just think you're . . ."

"Forget about it."

"No. No, I won't forget."

They look at each other for an instant. It is the look in Karen's eyes, more than the words, that makes Mallory's face go warm.

Mallory and Karen, divided by a gulf too wide for crossing, connect for one second. Then it is over, and Karen is Karen again, blonde and perfect, flouncing away with her swirling, bouncy walk.

Mallory stands still for a few seconds, confusion swarming in

her head, then proceeds down the hallway. The kids are all looking—not staring. Regarding.

She sees pity. She sees envy. She sees awe. She sees shock. She
sees fear.

She meets one pair of eyes after another, after another, after
another as she makes her way down the hall, turns the corner and
walks into Mr. Livingston's classroom.

ACKNOWLEDGEMENTS

Though writing a novel is a task that can be long and dauntingly lonely, I am fortunate to have a supporting cast of people in my life who consistently offer kindness, direction and a listening ear.

Bohdan Siedlecki is a humble, remarkable man who has provided me with guidance and inspiration and wisdom and support, giving me so much of his time and energy over the past nine years that I hardly know how to thank him (though I know he does not expect or require thanks).

My dear friend Margo Vandaelle reads all my manuscripts and offers thoughtful, insightful commentary, but more than that, she offers her love. In every way but blood, she is my sister.

My friend Bill Prouten kept nudging me along during those difficult times when I wondered if anyone would want to read Mallory's sometimes painful, angst-ridden story. The hardest task a writer faces each day is getting to the desk, and Bill helped me do that, day by day, until the novel was completed.

My wonderful agent and "fairy godmother" Sally Harding believed in this book from the beginning, understood it deeply, and persevered tirelessly until she found it the best possible home. My experience with the good people at Turnstone Press has been gratifying. I thank Todd Besant, Sharon Caseburg and Kelly Stifora for looking after my "baby" with such care. Wayne Tefs's sharp and discerning eye helped me flesh out thin spots, clarify my sometimes clouded vision, and hone the manuscript to a much more focussed point.

I could not do what I do without the constant and unwavering support of my wonderful family: my husband, my adult children and their partners. My daughter Shannon strongly believed that Mallory's story would have a life and a readership, a boost when the process became discouraging. The Gunning men are quietly steadfast in their love and support; I thank my son Jeff and my husband Bill for believing in me and my work, and loving me always. There is no greater gift.